"Is that what it takes to stop you?"

Elizabeth's voice was harsh as she continued. "Must I be wearing a ring to show previous ownership? Is that what it takes for you to leave me alone?"

"No, of course not," Quinn said impatiently, frowning. "Your grandfather told me there's nothing serious between you and Giles, so I—"

"Maybe you should have asked *me* that," she snapped in disgust. "Just because I'm not engaged doesn't mean I'm willing to fall into bed with the great star, Quinn Taylor!"

He drew a ragged breath. "If you want to deny you enjoyed that kiss, you can, but while you're deluding yourself, I'll know what really happened."

CAROLE MORTIMER, one of our most popular—and prolific—English authors, began writing for the Harlequin Presents series in 1979. She now has more than forty top-selling romances to her credit and shows no signs whatever of running out of plot ideas. She writes strong traditional romances with a distinctly modern appeal, and her winning way with characters and with romantic plot twists has earned her an enthusiastic audience worldwide.

Books by Carole Mortimer

Don't miss any of our special offers. Write to us at the following address for information on our newest releases.

Harlequin Reader Service
901 Fuhrmann Blvd., P.O. Box 1397, Buffalo, NY 14240
Canadian address: P.O. Box 603,
Fort Erie, Ont. L2A 5X3

CAROLE MORTIMER

wish for the moon

Harlequin Books

TORONTO • NEW YORK • LONDON
AMSTERDAM • PARIS • SYDNEY • HAMBURG
STOCKHOLM • ATHENS • TOKYO • MILAN

For John,
Matthew and Joshua

Harlequin Presents first edition June 1988
ISBN 0-373-11083-9

Original hardcover edition published in 1987
by Mills & Boon Limited

PROLOGUE

SHE felt a little like Cinderella must have done when she had her first glimpse of Prince Charming.

Not that the circumstances were quite the same: she didn't have two wicked stepsisters, only her cousin Fergus, but he could *definitely* be wicked! And although she had been orphaned at birth, her Aunt Madge was nothing like a wicked stepmother, and Uncle Hector could be very kind. Nevertheless, she had always known she was an interloper in the family, taken in because she was the daughter of Uncle Hector's sister, although no one had ever been cruel to her.

It had been a pleasant life, if uneventful, Uncle Hector making a meagre living tenant-farming on the Farnham estate.

It was because of *who* Quinn Taylor was that she suddenly felt as if she had been thrust into the midst of a fairy-tale.

With that ebony-dark hair, and those deep, deep-blue eyes, he had to be every woman's idea of a Prince Charming. And she hadn't even realised what sensuality was until she gazed upon Quinn Taylor. It surrounded him like an invisible aura, all the more potent because he seemed unaware of it. He was a lazily charming man who had had success after success singing about what he seemed to love best; the people he cared about, and the mountainous beauty that surrounded his Canadian home.

Canada's John Denver, he had been called, but from the moment Lise saw him she knew he was unique!

It was a fairy-tale that he was here in her aunt's and uncle's home at all. Her cousin Fergus had written a song that Quinn Taylor had been interested in recording for his next album. Fergus had been over the moon about the breakthrough, the biggest he had had since deciding to make song-writing his career, even more thrilled when the recording star asked him to sit in on the sessions at the London studio. Fergus's telephone conversations for the next week had been full of how wonderful the other man was, what a professional he was, and despite the fact that the other man was at least ten years older than Fergus's twenty-two the two of them seemd to have formed a friendship. Then had come the telephone call that had sent the Morrison household into an uproar.

Quinn Taylor had been staying at a hotel for the making of his next album, but somehow the Press and fans had found out where he was staying and besieged the place. Fergus had offered him the use of the spare bedroom at the Morrison farm, and to everyone's amazement he had accepted.

Aunt Madge had been in her element during the preparations for the star's arrival, having the whole house in turmoil during the two days, which was all the notice she had received from Fergus, paying little heed to her son's request for secrecy, telling everyone and anyone that Quinn Taylor was going to be a guest in *her* house. People had seemed slightly sceptical, but once the word got around that he had been seen at the house ...! Lise had a feeling his request for privacy was going to be short-lived.

The two men had arrived from the recording-studio shortly before dinner, Fergus's girlfriend Terri with them, Quinn Taylor very polite to them all, if slightly withdrawn during the meal.

Lise hadn't been able to take her eyes off him, knowing she was gawping like a schoolgirl, but unable to stop. Quinn Taylor was here, in *her* home, sitting at the dinner-table eating with *her* family.

Suddenly he looked up and met her gaze, smiling gently as he saw the guilty blush in her cheeks. 'I hope our late arrival hasn't made you too tired for dinner,' he smiled encouragingly.

Lise gave a pained frown. He thought she was still a child! Oh, she knew her tiny appearance often gave people that impression, and her Alice-in-Wonder-land hair, secured in a single braid down her spine tonight, didn't detract from the impression. But she liked having her hair long, and—and she wasn't a child, damn it!

Her resentment deepened as she sensed Terri's mocking glance on her. She and Terri had been at school together, Terri, at just twenty, her senior by three years, and she had never been able to understand what Fergus saw in the other girl. Apart from the obvious attractions, that was! Terri had begun modelling as soon as she left school at sixteen, and was relatively successful at it, a fact she never let anyone forget.

Lise knew that her own body still tended to run a little towards puppy-fat, but it was starting to go, her curves much more defined than they had been six months ago. She was just a late developer, her Uncle Hector had assured her when she voiced her concern to him. She had never wanted so desperately to appear older than her seventeen years than when she met Quinn Taylor, had worn the sundress that emphasised the fact that she was finally getting breasts and successfully hid the fact that her thighs were still a little more chunky than she would have wished. And it had all been for nothing; he thought she was a child up past her usual bedtime!

As if sensing that he had somehow committed a gaffe his smile deepened, and Lise stared at him in fascinated wonder.

'Fergus mentioned something about showing me his music-room after dinner.' Even his voice was sensual, deep and rich, the Canadian accent very attractive. 'Perhaps you would like to join us?' He quirked dark brows.

She glanced uncertainly at her aunt and uncle, knowing she had to help clear away after the meal, that it was one of her daily chores. But oh, how she longed to go with the other three to the loft over the cow-barn that had been converted into a music-room where Fergus could go and write without disturbing anyone.

Her uncle had converted the loft years ago, and when Fergus left to live in London three years ago he had told her she could use the room if she wanted to. It had become one of her favourite places, somewhere where she could be alone to think. And for the last two nights she had sat up there playing all her Quinn Taylor records, hardly able to believe that today he would be coming to stay with them. And now he had requested more of her company. Maybe she had misunderstood his last question; he certainly couldn't regard her as a child if he wanted to spend more time with her!

'Go ahead, love,' her uncle was the one to encourage. 'Your aunt and I can clear away here.'

'Oh, but——'

'Let the girl have some fun, Madge,' her uncle cut in firmly. 'It isn't as if she has much around here to distract her normally,' he added drily.

The farm was part of the thousands of acres owned by the Farnham family, part of the Hampshire estate, and with no close neighbours Lise usually spent her evenings reading in her room or listening to records. Occasionally she would go into town and go out with a couple of her friends, but mainly she just stayed at home.

'I wouldn't dream of leaving you to clear away,' Quinn Taylor spoke smoothly. 'Perhaps Lise and I can do the dishes for you?'

She blushed as he smiled at her encouragingly, loving the way he said her name, almost making it a caress. She wouldn't in the least mind doing the boring chore if she were going to be alone with Quinn Taylor in the kitchen!

'I wouldn't hear of it,' her aunt refused lightly. 'You all go on, Hector and I can manage here.'

Lise was well aware of the fact that it was only their guest's presence that was excusing her from doing the work; her aunt was usually very strict about the chores she had to do during the day, and washing-up after the meals was the least of them.

Given the unexpected freedom, Lise was the first one out of the house, all the time aware of the warm sensuality of the man who walked along behind her talking quietly to Fergus.

'Only another hour until your bedtime, isn't it?'

Lise's eyes flashed deeply green at the taunting voice of her cousin's girlfriend, turning to glare at her. 'The fact that I'm petite merely gives the illusion of my being young,' she returned, looking pointedly at the other girl's height, Terri being almost six feet tall.

Terri's mouth twisted. 'Try not to drool all over the poor man,' she mocked in a bored voice. 'I'm sure he doesn't want his shirt wet!'

Lise's cheeks were flushed at the barb, and she glanced uncomfortably behind them to see if the two men had heard their conversation; they were some way behind, still talking softly together.

Was her fascination with Quinn Taylor that obvious, or was Terri just being her usual bitchy self? Maybe it was a little of both, she realised ruefully, but could she help it if the man made her feel weak at the knees?

She had sat and gazed at one of his album covers last night, a close-up of his face as he smiled warmly into the camera. But the photograph hadn't been able to do justice to the silky thickness of his hair, or the sensual slumbrousness of those deep-blue eyes. And without the make-up that had obviously needed to be worn beneath the hot lights of the camera his skin was more rugged, his jaw square and firm. In the photograph he had been wearing a thick jumper but tonight he wore a royal-blue shirt unbuttoned at the throat to reveal the start of the dark hair that no doubt covered most of his chest, his denims snug to his hips and thighs; Fergus had obviously warned him there would be no dressing up for dinner in the Morrison household, no matter who their guest was. He looked as if he were more comfortable in his casual clothes than he could ever have been in a formal suit, anyway.

Could she help it if he was much more devastating in the flesh than he was on an album cover or on television? And couldn't she be excused for staring at him a little? Damn Terri for making her so self-conscious that she was afraid even to glance at him now!

The loft ran the whole length of the cow-barn, the roof reinforced to take the weight of the piano that stood near the floor-length window, the other end of the room converted to a lounge, with a stereo system wired up there.

Quinn grinned at Fergus as he picked up the top three albums in the pile. 'I can't fault your taste in music,' he drawled, all three albums his.

Fergus grinned back, as sandy-haired as his father, although happily neither had the freckles that often went with that colouring. His laughing blue eyes were warm with laughter. 'All the Quinn Taylor albums you'll find there are Lise's,' he admitted softly. 'I only became a fan because she played your music so much it was either that or go insane!'

Lise blushed uncomfortably as Quinn turned to her questioningly. 'Your songs are so—real,' she said awkwardly. 'They often make me cry.'

His expression gentled. 'I'm sorry. I never like to be responsible for making a lovely lady cry.'

She shrugged. 'I only cry because the songs are so beautiful.'

'Thank you,' he accepted huskily.

Lise stared at him, mesmerised. And somehow she knew that not all of the lines beside his eyes had been caused by laughter, that he had known his share of sadness too.

Of course he had known sadness, she mentally rebuked herself, hadn't his wife of ten years left him last summer, taking their daughter with her? For a long time there had been rumours of a reconciliation, but now those rumours were suggesting there would in fact be a divorce instead. Considering some of Quinn's best songs were about the happiness he had known with his family this had to be a deep blow to him.

'How about we make our own music?' Fergus lightly cut in on the awkward moment, acknowledging Lise's grateful smile with a conspiratorial wink. 'Quinn?' he indicated the piano as he picked up his guitar for himself.

'And what do we play?' Terri drawled as she leant gracefully against the piano.

'You can use Lise's guitar.' He handed it to her with a grin, patting the stool beside his. 'And Lise can share the piano with Quinn.'

She swallowed hard as Quinn moved accommodatingly along the bench stool, sitting gingerly beside him, her pulse racing at his proximity.

But her awkwardness left her after several minutes, as she struggled to keep up with Fergus as he moved from one sing-along song to another, the sensuously slender hands that moved along the keys beside her own distracting her from paying full attention to what she was doing. Quinn had lovely hands, long and thin, with tiny dark hairs covering the backs of his fingers. He made her own tiny hands look childlike, making her fully aware of how forcefully muscular he was.

And she was fascinated as he sang a rowdy song with Fergus, able to recognise that his voice was as true now as it was on his albums.

Suddenly he turned and once again caught her staring at him, sharing a grin with her before turning back to her cousin. Lise felt as if someone had struck her in the chest.

She was in love! Fully, completely, utterly, in love with Quinn Taylor. And now that he knew she wasn't a child he seemed to like her too!

She, Lise Morrison, who had never had a boyfriend in her life, was in love with Quinn Taylor, a man who was known worldwide for his wonderful singing talent, who grossed millions every year in revenue from his songs and albums. It was incredible. Wonderful. It was impossible!

She was seventeen, he was thirty-two; he was still married, even if he was getting a divorce.

She felt so deflated she could have cried. As it was she played all the completely wrong notes, breaking off apologetically as Quinn turned to her with gentle enquiry.

Fergus broke off too as he sensed her distress. 'Terri and I will go over to the house and get some beers,' he suggested lightly. 'We need it after all that singing.' His arm was about Terri's shoulders as they left to go over to the house.

Lise knew she should move away from Quinn, that her emotions were too vulnerable sitting this close to him.

He turned towards her, leaning his arm on the top of the piano. 'I'm sorry if I embarrassed you earlier,' he spoke gruffly. 'Fergus had mentioned his little cousin to me,' he shrugged. 'And I——'

'It's all right,' she hastily dismissed. 'I *am* little.'

His lips curved into a gentle smile. 'How old are you?'

'Seventeen,' she supplied reluctantly,

His eyes widened, and she realised she had surprised him. How old had he thought she was, for goodness' sake!

'Two days ago,' she added heavily.

Again his eyes widened. 'I had no idea . . . I should have brought you something,' he shrugged.

'Why?' She blinked up at him, fascinated by how clear a blue his eyes were this close, his lashes thick and dark.

He frowned slightly, staring back at her, both of them suddenly breathing very shallowly. 'Lise——' He began to shake his head.

She moved slightly closer to him on the bench-seat. 'If you really want to give me a present . . .' she prompted breathlessly.

'Yes?' The slightly up-and-down movement of his chest as he breathed almost brought him into contact with her breasts.

She blinked once, closer still. 'You could kiss me,' she encouraged huskily.

He moved back slightly. 'No, Lise, I——' He couldn't protest any more because she had launched herself into his arms, her arms about his neck as she kissed him with all the love inside her she had just discovered for him.

It was wonderful, his lips warm and firm beneath her own. She clung to him mindlessly, totally unprepared for the way his hand dug into her nape as he threaded his fingers into her plait there and dragged her painfully away from him.

His eyes glittered down into hers, his mouth a taut line. 'What the hell do you think you're doing?' he rasped.

Consternation washed over her as she became completely aware of exactly what she *had* done. This man was here as Fergus's guest, had shown her politeness but nothing else, and she had just thrown herself at him!

His expression softened as he saw the tears glistening in her eyes. 'You should have waited for the invitation, little one,' he told her softly. 'This is the way I like to kiss.' He gently parted her lips before lowering his head to hers, the way he kissed so much more than the tight-lipped caress she had given him.

As his lips continued to move against hers she felt as if she had become a part of him, melded to him, following his lead, realising that until this moment she had known nothing about a kiss at all. She felt as if she were being consumed!

He moved back abruptly as Fergus and Terri could be heard returning up the stairs. 'Happy birthday,' he murmured gruffly, standing up to move away from her, his hands thrust into his denims pockets as he stared out across the countryside.

'Think you'll be able to stand the quiet for another couple of weeks?' Terri drawled, moving to stand next to him, handing him an open can of beer.

He turned to her slightly. 'I was brought up in Alberta, on a wheat farm my parents refuse to leave. I don't think I'll ever stop being a country boy,' he added a little wistfully.

Lise just sat and watched him, his profile firm and dominant in the last of dusk's shadows. Her heart was pounding, her hands trembling. Quinn Taylor had just kissed her. Oh, she had asked him to, and the first time she had taken the initiative, but that last kiss Quinn had controlled completely. If Fergus and Terri hadn't returned when they had . . .

'Here you are, Squirt.' Fergus handed her a can of Coke, sitting beside her on the piano bench. 'Mum says you ought to be going in,' he added regretfully. 'You have an early start in the morning.'

She looked uncomfortably at Quinn, but he was still staring out into the rapidly darkening night. Maybe he hadn't heard her being ordered to bed as if she were still a little girl; she certainly hoped so!

But her aunt was right about the early start. She had been helping her uncle with his summer crops during her break between finishing school and starting college when the new term began. Farm work was long and hard, but her uncle needed the help, and the money he was able to pay her was more than welcome. Just last week she had bought another Quinn Taylor album with some of her wages.

'I'll go in now,' she nodded, smoothing down her dress as she stood up. 'Goodnight, Terri,' she called to the other girl. 'Goodnight—Quinn.' She refused to call him *Mr* Taylor after he had kissed her so thoroughly.

The bleakness left his eyes as he turned to her. 'Goodnight, Lise,' he returned gruffly.

She smiled at him shyly. 'I—I'll see you tomorrow.'

He nodded abruptly, his expression giving away none of his thoughts.

'How about a kiss goodnight, Squirt?' Fergus teased as she would have turned to leave.

For a moment she looked at Quinn blankly, and then she realised Fergus wanted her to kiss *him* goodnight, not the other man.

'Of course.' Embarrassed colour darkened her cheeks as she bent to kiss her cousin on the cheek. 'Goodnight, Fergus.' She smiled at him shakily.

''Night, button.' He returned the smile.

She and Fergus had always been the best of friends, her cousin feeling none of the resentment towards her that so many other children might have done when a new baby suddenly invades their home, especially as that baby wasn't actually a brother or sister. Or maybe it was because of that, because he had always realised she would never usurp his place with his parents. Whatever the reason Fergus had always loved her, always protected her. He couldn't possibly realise that he had just introduced her to the biggest danger she had ever known in her young life!

She was in love, irrevocably, and Quinn hadn't kissed her as if he hated her either.

Her aunt and uncle were still in the lounge, and she bade them a dreamy goodnight, making her way slowly up to bed, glancing longingly towards the closed door of the guest bedroom that she knew Quinn would be occupying later tonight. Only a wall would separate them, her room next to his. Would he think of her, and that kiss they had shared, as she thought of him?

Quinn Taylor, the man she had fantasised about for years, had kissed her, actually kissed *her*, Lise Morrison.

No one would ever believe it. *She* didn't believe it!

She danced around her bedroom in delight, as light as a butterfly, for once not minding that she was so tiny, and not quite as slim as she might have been. Quinn hadn't seemed to mind, so why should she?

Of course, if he wanted her to slim, she would. She would do anything he wanted her to, anything. She belonged to him now, wanted to spend the rest of her life with him. And he wanted her too, she was sure of it.

She danced around the bedroom again, singing to herself, feeling as light as air, discarding one nightdress after another as she realised each was too childish for her to wear. She wasn't a child any longer, she was a woman, and in future she was going to act and dress like one.

The first thing she was going to do was throw out all her old clothes, she couldn't go around looking like a child when a man like Quinn Taylor wanted her.

As a first step towards changing the clothes she wore she wasn't going to wear anything to sleep in in future; sleeping nude certainly ought to be mature enough!

She came to an abrupt halt as she wondered if Quinn slept nude too, her heart pounding in her chest as she envisaged him lying beneath a sheet, his nakedness clearly defined beneath the flimsy covering. His skin would be dark; the little she had seen of it had been. He would be tanned all over, firm flesh, taut muscles, with a feline beauty. She had goose-bumps just thinking about Quinn lying in bed!

She moved to the window, her bedroom overlooking the yard, staring across at the music-room, able to see Quinn as he laughed and talked with Fergus and Terri. He would be coming to bed soon himself, for the three of them were even now clearing up the debris from the evening.

Lise was filled with such a longing to be with Quinn tonight, wanted him so badly she trembled at the thought of lying in his arms. But Terri would be sharing her room for the night, and she dared not risk the other woman realising she had gone to Quinn. Perhaps after Terri had gone to Fergus ...

She deliberately pretended to already be asleep when the other girl came to bed, keeping her back firmly turned towards the room, knowing that once Terri was sure no one would hear her she would creep across the hallway to Fergus's room for the night. Her aunt and uncle wouldn't hear of Fergus sleeping with his girlfriend under their roof, but

Lise had known for some time that Terri crept out of their bedroom as soon as she was sure the rest of the family were asleep. And tonight when Terri went to Fergus she intended going to Quinn.

She could hear him in the next room now, not all that well, because the walls of this old cottage were thick, but she knew the man she loved was just through the thickness of that wall. What a surprise he was going to get when she went to him . . .!

Just over half an hour later all that could be heard in the room was the steady tick-tock of Lise's bedside clock. Her breathing sounded abnormally loud to her in the silence of the night, but only she seemed aware of it, Terri moving about the room putting on her robe.

'Lise?' she prompted softly, testingly.

She didn't move, although her heart seemed to be pounding very loudly too.

'Lise?' Terri called again, sighing her satisfaction as Lise remained turned away from her, seemingly asleep.

She waited only seconds after the door closed behind the other girl before quickly getting out of bed herself, shivering slightly in her nude state; sleeping without clothes on was certainly going to take some getting used to! The coolness of these cottages wasn't meant for sleeping nude. She gratefully pulled on her robe, belting it before going out into the hallway, moving stealthily to the door next to hers, coming to a freezing halt as she heard Quinn talking to someone inside his room, the door not quite closed properly.

'—told you in London, this has to stop,' Quinn

was saying firmly.

'Because of Fergus,' Terri acknowledged softly. 'But he doesn't have to know, does he?' she dismissed.

Terri was in Quinn's room. Lise couldn't believe it. Terri had gone to *Quinn*, not to Fergus!

She couldn't move, could hardly breathe, shocked to the core of her being.

Quinn sighed. 'He's a friend of mine——'

'I won't tell him if you don't,' Terri taunted seductively.

'He's expecting you to go to him——'

'I'll just tell him Lise made a little pest of herself by not falling asleep in time,' Terri said callously. 'She is a little pest, isn't she, Quinn?' she added derisively. 'The poor little thing can hardly keep her hands off you!'

'Terri——'

'Don't try and tell me you found her adoration cute—or acceptable,' Terri dismissed with a throaty laugh. 'We both know your opinion of star-struck little kids like her. You like a woman in your arms and your bed. And we both know that I'm very much a woman, don't we, Quinn?' she prompted huskily.

'Obviously you're a woman. But——'

'Let me show you how much of a woman I am,' Terri cut in seductively.

The silence that followed her statement broke Lise out of her horrified trance as she realised exactly *how* Terri must be *showing* Quinn.

She couldn't get back to her bedroom fast

enough, leaning weakly back against the door, her breathing ragged.

Terri and Quinn. Quinn was making love to the other woman while his friend, and Terri's lover, slept unsuspectingly across the hallway!

She had believed Quinn was attracted to her because he let her kiss him, because he had shown her what a proper kiss between a man and a woman could be, and all the time he was sleeping with his friend's girlfriend behind his back. Maybe Terri's presence here as Fergus's girlfriend had even been the reason he had been so agreeable to the suggestion that he stay here.

As for Quinn finding *her* attractive, that was laughable. Maybe he and Terri would indeed laugh later when he told her how Lise had thrown herself at him in the music-room!

She gave a sudden shiver, realising how cold she was standing here in just her robe, and, taking one of the cotton nightgowns that buttoned to the throat from her drawer, she pulled it on quickly, no longer eager to become a woman.

Oh God, Quinn wasn't a Prince Charming at all, he was the Prince who woke Sleeping Beauty with a single kiss, who opened her eyes to all that was ugly in the world.

She might not *want* to be a woman any more, but she knew for certain that she would never again be that trustingly naïve child who believed in fairy-tales. In men like Quinn Taylor . . .

CHAPTER ONE

'MISS ELIZABETH?'

She looked up from the letter of acceptance she had been writing in answer to a dinner invitation for next week, nodding coolly to the maid. 'Yes, Mary?' she prompted distantly.

'Cook just wanted to be sure that the number for lunch is still four.' The young maid looked at her eagerly.

Elizabeth put down her pen, smiling ruefully. 'Assure Cook that so far my grandfather's guests haven't cancelled their luncheon appointment,' she drawled, glancing at the gold watch her grandfather, Gerald Farnham, had given her for her twenty-first birthday two years ago. 'And as it's after eleven now I think we can *all* safely assume that they aren't going to either,' she added teasingly.

Mary blushed. She was only four years younger than her mistress, but so much younger in her outlook on life. 'Fancy Quinn Taylor coming here for lunch,' she breathed ecstatically, her eyes glowing with anticipation.

Elizabeth gave a dismissive shrug. 'One assumes he still has to eat like us lesser mortals,' she derided, glancing down at the half-finished letter. She didn't particularly want to go to the Prestwicks' for dinner, but Giles, the man she was currently dating, would want to go.

'But he's actually coming *here*,' Mary repeated excitedly, in no hurry to return to the kitchen.

Elizabeth was well aware of the fact that the singer was coming here, that even now the west lawn of the estate was having a stage and lighting erected on it in preparation for the concert her grandfather had agreed to let Quinn Taylor perform there.

A pop concert wasn't the sort of thing her grandfather would usually have agreed to, but the amount of money offered in return for the use of Farnham Hall for the televised concert had been too good for him to turn down. And her grandfather was all for making money where possible, she acknowledged ruefully. Besides which, he had tied the Quinn Taylor organisation up in so tight a contract that the west lawn and surrounding estate would probably be in a better condition when all the people and equipment were gone than it had been before they arrived! Her grandfather was nothing if not a good businessman.

Entertaining the pop singer and his manager for lunch wasn't something Elizabeth exactly relished doing, but her grandfather had believed it would make for good relations between them. She had a sneaking suspicion he might also be a Quinn Taylor fan!

Apparently the singer had arrived in England late last night and expected to begin rehearsing the show this afternoon; her grandfather had decided that the least they could do was offer him lunch before he began. She just hoped she didn't have to suffer through having him ask the entertainer for his autograph!

'Shouldn't you go and assure Cook that so far Mr Taylor hasn't cancelled the arrangements?' she drily prompted the young maid.

Mary looked at her consideringly. 'I'd be a nervous wreck if I were the one shortly to be having lunch with Quinn Taylor,' she sighed dreamily.

'Well, you aren't,' Elizabeth said more sharply than she intended, sighing as Mary looked hurt by her attitude. 'I'm sorry, Mary,' she dismissed. 'But there are several other things I would rather be doing today than having lunch with Mr Taylor.'

'I'd give a whole year's wages just to be able to say I spoke to him,' Mary said longingly.

Considering that the wages paid to the household staff at the Hall were some of the highest in the area, Mary's sacrifice wouldn't be a small one, and all for the opportunity to talk to a man who probably didn't deserve her hero-worship in the first place.

She gave the young girl a rueful smile. 'Tell Cook I said you were to help serve lunch today—without sacrifice of wages,' she added teasingly.

Mary's face lit up as if the lights on a Christmas tree had just been switched on. 'Really?' she gasped disbelievingly.

'As long as you don't mind going off for your own lunch now so that you can be back in time,' she nodded.

Mary's eyes were wide brown orbs. 'I don't mind not having any lunch at all if I can just get to see Quinn Taylor close up,' she said weakly.

Elizabeth smiled. 'Run along and get your lunch

now. You wouldn't want to faint at Mr Taylor's feet, now would you?' she teased, suddenly sure that the enchanted girl would enjoy nothing better than fainting in Quinn Taylor's arms. 'On second thoughts, perhaps you would,' she acknowledged drily. 'But don't, hm?' she prompted gently.

'No, Miss Elizabeth.' The young girl left with a dreamy smile to her lips.

Elizabeth shook her head, gazing out of the window of the morning-room to where she could see the west lawn in the distance as the crew frantically worked to finish the staging in time for the concert at the weekend.

All that work and adoration for a man who undoubtedly had a good voice, but who was still just a man after all. Personally, she didn't understand what all the fuss was about, although the thousands of Quinn Taylor fans who were said to be going to attend the concert obviously thought that they did.

But she wasn't the only one who wasn't exactly overjoyed about the invasion planned for the weekend; Giles was disgusted that her grandfather could even be thinking of allowing such a thing at the Hall. She smiled a little as she remembered that her grandfather hadn't been too thrilled by the criticism. If Giles had serious thoughts about becoming her husband and Gerald Farnham's grandson-in-law then he would do well to learn that her grandfather disliked criticism of any sort, was just as likely to do something he wouldn't normally have done just because someone suggested he shouldn't.

And she was pretty certain that Giles did have

serious intentions of asking her to marry him. What her answer to him was going to be when he did ask she hadn't yet decided. Oh, he was a nice enough man, quite good-looking with his curly blond hair and dark brown eyes that could look so soulful, but she wasn't sure yet whether or not she was in love with him. But there was no rush to decide, they had only been going out together for a few months. She was certainly in no hurry to marry anyone.

'Darling, isn't it time you changed for lunch?' her grandfather prompted softly from the doorway. 'Our guests should be arriving in half an hour or so, and for some reason it seems to take you women at least that long to change a few clothes,' he added drily.

Elizabeth turned to smile at her grandfather, giving up any idea of being able to deal with her mail any further today. None of it was that important anyway. 'I thought I looked fine as I am,' she drawled, standing up to cross the room and kiss him on one leathery cheek.

At almost seventy her grandfather still stood straight and tall at just over six feet, his hair deeply thick and iron-grey, hazel eyes twinkling down at her with affection as he held her at arm's length to take in her appearance.

'You look charming—as usual, my dear,' he said lightly, about the pink floral dress. 'But I had something a little more—formal in mind, for the mistress of the house,' he added encouragingly.

'I doubt a Canadian pop-singer knows the difference between a Laura Ashley and a St Laurent,' she said drily.

Her grandfather gave her a reproving look. 'That wasn't worthy of you, Elizabeth,' he told her softly.

'No,' she sighed heavily, putting her arm through the crook of his as they walked out into the large entrance-hall. 'I just wish you had excused me from this luncheon as I asked you to,' she grimaced. 'I have no idea what we're going to talk about. It isn't even as if I'm a fan,' she shrugged.

'No doubt the man talks about himself all the time,' her grandfather derided.

She looked up to return his smile. 'If he does it will save me having to try and make conversation!'

'Minx!' he chuckled.

She ran lightly to the foot of the wide stairway. 'I promise to try not to embarrass you.'

'Elizabeth,' he stopped her as she reached the gallery at the top of the stairs. 'You could never, ever embarrass me,' he told her gruffly.

She gave him a warm smile, blowing him a kiss before hurrying to her bedroom.

She and her grandfather were so close, and that closeness was another reason she was in no hurry to think about marriage; she was all her grandfather had now, since his son, her father, had been killed five years ago while racing his car at over a hundred miles an hour. She and her grandfather had been drawn together after the tragedy, their affection for each other something really special. A husband would surely try to intrude upon that special relationship; Giles had already shown signs of impatience at the amount of time she chose to spend at home.

After years of knowing exactly what was right to

wear for each and every occasion, she was suddenly at a loss as to what one wore to have lunch with a pop-singer, disgarding one outfit after another in her wardrobe as either too formal or too casual. What *could* she wear to have lunch with Quinn Taylor and his manager?

It wasn't like her to be so indecisive. Surely she wasn't as affected by the man's expected arrival as everyone else seemed to be? Certainly not, she instantly answered herself, she was just irritated at having to put herself out for the man!

She chose her outfit at random from the row of day clothes in the full-wall-length wardrobe and was just zipping the green skirt over her slender hips when she heard the sound of a car in the driveway; she tucked the matching pale green blouse into the narrow waistband before moving to glance out of the window. If it was Quinn Taylor he was early, but perhaps no one had bothered to explain to him that it was just as rude to arrive early as it was to arrive late.

The Rolls-Royce that had just come to a stop in front of the house was certainly impressive enough—if one were the type to be impressed by such an obvious show of wealth, which Elizabeth certainly was not.

She watched curiously from the window as instead of the chauffeur alighting from behind the wheel as she had expected, a tall dark-haired man in his late thirties, instantly recognisable as Quinn Taylor, stepped out on to the gravel driveway. Even if he hadn't been, it was obvious that the short, slightly plump man who was getting out of the passenger side certainly wasn't the singing star, which meant he must be the manager, Bruce Simons.

The shorter man walked around the car to join Quinn Taylor, pointing across the grounds to the west lawn where work was visibly in progress.

Elizabeth observed them curiously, noting that Bruce Simons seemed slightly ill at ease in the brown suit he wore, obviously especially for the occasion, pulling at the restriction of the collar of the tan shirt as it obviously irritated him.

Quinn Taylor turned to grin at him as he said something, wearing his navy blue suit with ease, even from this distance his eyes distinguisable as a deep startling blue. He seemed relaxed, confident, motioning to the other man that they should go into the house now.

Elizabeth stepped back from the window as they turned towards the house; the last thing she wanted was to be caught staring at them like some star-struck idiot!

She should be getting downstairs, her grand-father wouldn't be pleased if she weren't downstairs at his side to greet their guests. One thing she had learnt about her grandfather over the years, he granted her every indulgence, but good manners meant everything to him. He was going to expect her to be especially polite to a man he admired so much.

She brushed the shoulder-length bell of her hair with quick strokes, aware that she looked coolly elegant, her eyes sparkling brightly.

Petersham was just showing their guests into the

drawing-room as she descended the stairs, and she turned coolly towards them as she sensed someone's gaze on her, her gaze meeting, and clashing, with that of Quinn Taylor.

His eyes widened speculatively, a slow sensuous smile curving his sculptured lips. And then, as he continued to meet her challenging gaze, puzzlement darkened his eyes.

Elizabeth finished descending the stairs with confident dignity, crossing the entrance-hall to smile politely at their guests. 'Thank you, Petersham,' she dismissed the butler lightly. 'I'll take our guests through to my grandfather. Would you like to come this way, gentlemen,' she invited politely, her smile bright—and completely meaningless, sensing that Quinn Taylor's gaze was still on her. 'I'm Elizabeth Farnham, by the way,' she told them distantly as she ushered them into the room where her grandfather stood waiting for them. 'Mr Simon, I believe you know my grandfather already.' She smiled at the plump man, aware that he had been the one to do all the negotiating with her grandfather. 'Mr Taylor, my grandfather, Gerald Farnham,' she introduced. 'I don't believe you need any introduction yourself,' she added drily, moving slightly away from the group to observe them uninterestedly.

Her grandfather was obviously enthusiastic about meeting the singer for the first time. As she had suspected, he was a secret fan, mentioning several of the entertainer's songs that he particularly liked.

'I'm afraid our introduction was a little rushed earlier.' A silkily soft voice broke into her rueful musings.

She looked up to find Quinn Taylor had left the other two men talking quietly together to cross the room to her side. She met his gaze questioningly, smiling politely.

'Elizabeth Farnham,' she provided again as he looked at her searchingly.

'Elizabeth ...' he repeated softly, shaking his head. 'No, it doesn't—fit,' he murmured slowly.

She gave a lightly dismissive laugh. 'I can assure you it suits me very well,' she challenged.

He looked slightly embarrassed. 'I'm sorry.' He gave a tight smile. 'I didn't mean to appear rude. It's just ... You remind me of someone, it's almost as if I should know you, and yet the name Elizabeth doesn't ring any bells in my memory.' He shook his head, staring at her intently.

'I'm sorry,' she drawled dismissively, moving to join her grandfather, putting her arm through the crook of his, glancing back curiously at Quinn Taylor. He still stared at her. 'Mr Taylor seems to think I may have a double somewhere,' she told her grandfather with a light laugh.

He turned to the younger man. 'I refuse to believe there's another woman as beautiful as Elizabeth anywhere in the world,' and he gazed down at her proudly.

Quinn Taylor strode fluidly across the room. 'I didn't say you have a double, Miss Farnham,' he bit out, obviously not appreciating her mockery at his expense. 'I said *you* remind me of someone.'

'Surely it's the same thing?' she dismissed uninterestedly. 'I can assure you that if we had met before I would surely have remembered it—even if you are so ungallant as to suggest you can't remember where you met this woman I look so much like,' she added challengingly.

Impatience flickered in his eyes, at himself—and her. 'Perhaps I was mistaken,' he rasped. 'You don't appear to be the sort of woman a man *would* easily forget.'

'I certainly hope not,' she drawled huskily.

It was a most unnerving feeling having someone watch her so closely as she ate, and yet she knew, without acknowledging it, that Quinn Taylor watched her constantly during lunch.

Just as Mary watched him. The poor girl helped serve the meal in a complete daze, even dropping the spoon on the floor when Quinn Taylor turned to thank her for taking his empty soup bowl away. The accident cost Mary a quelling glance from Petersham, making her especially careful throughout the rest of the meal.

She really was star-struck, poor girl, gazing after Quinn Taylor adoringly as they finally left the dining-room to have coffee in the drawing-room.

'Brandy, gentlemen?' her grandfather offered, not bothering himself when the other two men declined. 'Any problems, Quinn,' he told the other man effusively as he sat down to light himself one of the cigars he so enjoyed and which Elizabeth was always warning him were no good for him, 'and I want you to come straight to me.' He puffed on his cigar. 'I'd be glad to help in any way that I can.'

She could instantly tell that her grandfather didn't just like the man's music, he liked the man too. When her grandfather decided he liked someone he would do anything he could to make things easier for them, but woe betide anyone he took a dislike to!

Quinn smiled his lazily charming smile, seeming to be giving her a respite from his constant attention. 'Everything seems to be running smoothly, thanks, Gerald.' The two men had quickly come to a first-name basis. 'Although perhaps there is something Miss Farnham could help me with.' The two of *them* hadn't reached the same easy familiarity!

She stiffened, her gaze cool. 'Yes?'

'The perfume you're wearing,' he said softly. 'Perhaps you could give me the name of it before I leave,' he explained as her brows rose questioningly. 'I'd like to buy someone some like it as a present.'

'Of course,' she agreed distantly, wondering how many 'someones' he intended buying the expensive perfume for. Since his divorce several years ago he had gained the reputation of escorting some of the most beautiful women in the entertainment business. 'I'll write the name down for you before you leave,' she drawled.

He gave an inclination of his head. 'I'd be grateful.'

Elizabeth broke the intimacy of his gaze by turning towards her grandfather. 'Perhaps Mr Taylor would like to go over to the west lawn now and see how the work there is progressing,' she suggested lightly. 'I'm sure he must be anxious to see what arrangements have been made.'

'He's barely had time to drink his coffee, child,' her grandfather looked at her in surprise.

She blushed. 'I only——'

'Your granddaughter is right, Gerald,' Quinn Taylor's drawling voice came to her rescue. 'I only have a couple of days' rehearsal before the concert.' He stood up, stretching lazily. 'I don't feel much like working after that delicious lunch you just gave us,' he acknowledged ruefully. 'Maybe I can return the hospitality some time, tomorrow, perhaps?' He was looking at Elizabeth as he made the suggestion. After angering her grandfather by more or less suggesting it was time for the singer and his manager to leave, she prudently held her tongue about bluntly refusing Quinn Taylor's invitation. But she certainly had no intention of spending any more time in his company than she had to, she didn't like the way he kept staring at her.

To her relief it was Bruce Simons who came to her rescue, pointing out to the singer that the schedule was a little tight for tomorrow.

Blue eyes gleamed as Quinn Taylor seemed to know of her relief at the reprieve. 'Maybe we can make it dinner,' he murmured slowly. 'Could I contact you both about it tomorrow?' he asked her grandfather.

He might contact them, but by the time he did she would make sure she had a legitimate excuse—one that would satisfy her grandfather!—for not attending. Quinn Taylor made her feel uncomfortable, and she wasn't about to expose herself to any more of his company than she had to.

'It's been a delight to meet you, Miss Farnham.' He took her hand lightly in his as they stood outside. 'I'm sure I will remember who it is you remind me of,' he added softly, once again giving her that searching look.

'Let's hope that when you do remember, it is a pleasant memory,' she drawled mockingly.

He smiled, his teeth white and even against his bronzed skin. 'I'm sure it must be,' he said huskily.

Elizabeth politely but firmly extricated her hand from within his grasp, knowing by the way his fingers tightened momentarily that he didn't want to release her. She clasped her hands together in front of her. 'We mustn't keep you from your rehearsal any longer,' she said pointedly.

'No,' he acknowledged ruefully, strolling around to the driver's side of the car with long easy movements. 'I'll see you both again soon.'

It sounded more like a threat than a politely made parting comment. But she knew her grandfather would want to accept this man's invitation, whereas she didn't believe it was necessary for them to meet again, for dinner tomorrow or anything else, now that they had politely done their duty.

They stood at the top of the steps watching the car as it disappeared in the direction of the west lawn, her grandfather's arm about her shoulders as they went back into the house.

'You weren't very polite to him, darling,' her grandfather finally reproved, as she had known he would.

'His approach wasn't very original,' she derided. 'That "you remind me of someone" routine must be years old,' she dismissed scathingly.

'It used to work when I was a young man,' he frowned. 'OK, point taken,' he smiled as she gave him a pointed look. 'But it didn't seem like an approach to me.'

'Perhaps not,' she shrugged. 'But I didn't like the way he kept staring at me through lunch.'

Her grandfather smiled again. 'He did seem rather taken with you, didn't he?'

'There's no need to sound so smug,' Elizabeth snapped. 'Quinn Taylor is certainly not my type!'

'Because he sings for a living?' her grandfather frowned. 'Darling, the man is an artist, not some hack who can't pitch a note!'

Elizabeth knew exactly who Quinn Taylor was, and *what* he was. The Lise Morrison part of her would never forget that he had taken to his bed the girlfriend of a man who had called him friend.

Or that he had once broken her heart.

CHAPTER TWO

ELIZABETH didn't for a moment believe he really remembered that slightly overweight schoolgirl who had once been so infatuated with him that she had thrown herself at him shamelessly.

But she remembered every painful moment of that night six years ago. She had thought she had put it behind her, had believed seeing Quinn Taylor again after all this time would mean nothing to her. But she had been wrong; how could anyone forget the person who had shattered their childhood for ever?

At seventeen she had been extremely naïve, believed everything to be exactly as it appeared to be: Quinn's kindness to her a sign that he liked her too, his friendship with Fergus just that. Instead it had merely been a cover for something much more sordid. Terri hadn't returned to her bedroom until early the next morning!

Quinn said she reminded him of someone, but the name was all wrong. Maybe it was just a line to him, but for her it had been a traumatic experience to learn that she wasn't little Lise Morrison at all but Elizabeth Farnham, heiress to the Farnham estate.

She had been eighteen when the man her Uncle Hector called 'Master Gregory', had been killed racing one of his cars much too fast during wet conditions. The people in the area had mourned the loss of the Farnham heir with the elderly man who owned most of the farms and houses they lived in. For days they had been stunned by the death, wondering what Gerald Farnham would do for an heir now that his only son had died, Gregory Farnham never having married himself.

Elizabeth could still remember her surprise—and nervousness!—when the Farnham limousine had arrived at the farm and Gerald Farnham himself had asked to see *her*.

His son had left a letter to be read in the event of his premature death—and with the reckless way he lived his life that had always been more than a possibility—stating that he and Claire Morrison had been lovers, and claiming Lise's paternity.

The man who claimed to be her grandfather had shown her the letter, not attempting to shield her from the fact that her father had always known of her existence, that he had scorned her mother when she told him of her pregnancy. It hadn't been easy to accept that, if Gregory Farnham hadn't died the way he had, she would never have known who she really was; that the secret of her father's identity, which her mother had chosen to take to the grave with her, would have remained a secret for ever.

Her mother had gone to live with her brother Hector when their parents died shortly after she was sixteen, and she and Gregory Farnham had met when she was only seventeen. Considering the reputation the Farnham heir had always had concerning women, Lise could only believe that her

mother had been as mesmerised by his reckless
charm as so many other women had seemed to be.
But at only nineteen Gregory Farnham had had no
intention of marrying anyone, especially some little
country bumpkin who lived on one of the estate's
farms, even if she was pregnant with his child.

Her aunt and uncle had been as stunned by this
revelation as she was, and she was sure they had
never had any idea who her father was. Her Aunt
Madge certainly wouldn't have remained silent if
she had known!

It had been too much for Lise to absorb, and she
had run off, needing to be alone, to try to come to
terms with the fact that she was Elizabeth *Farnham*
and not Elizabeth Morrison.

Her poor mother, rejected by the man she had
believed loved her. Not even her death had made
him relent about acknowledging their child's birth.

Maybe if she had been able to comfort herself
with the certainty that Gregory Farnham had lived
his life so recklessly *because* the woman he had loved,
and foolishly hadn't married, had died giving birth
to his child, there might have been something to
redeem from the heartache she was now suffering.
But that *would* have been a fairy-tale, and her belief
in those had been shattered a year ago.

In which case she had to believe that her father
had been a selfish bastard who had never had any
intention of recognising her as his daughter while he
was still alive. To her he had just been the Farnham
heir who occasionally visited the estate, driving
about the narrow country lanes in one of his flashy

sports cars, usually with some beautiful woman at his side.

She didn't want him to be her father, hated the thought of that blond-haired devil having sired her. She *didn't* have to accept him as her father if she didn't want to. She knew her aunt and uncle expected her to move into Farnham Hall as her grandfather wanted her to, but she was eighteen now, could go where she wanted, be what she wanted. She didn't have to be beholden to anyone any more——

'He was a bastard, wasn't he.'

She looked up with resentful eyes, glaring at the man who now claimed to be her grandfather. He had a perfect right to be here, this river was part of his estate, but she didn't have to stay and talk to him.

He caught her arm as she would have leapt up and run away. 'Lise,' he halted her gently. 'That is what they call you, isn't it?' he prompted softly.

Her head went back defiantly, green eyes flashing. 'It's the family name for me, yes,' she acknowledged bitterly.

He nodded his head, a man in his mid-sixties who was obviously finding it difficult to converse with a young woman. 'If you prefer I'll call you Elizabeth,' he said sadly. 'But I *am* your family.' His hand tightened about her arm as she would have pulled away. 'You know, I used to see your mother about the village and estate,' he spoke quietly. 'She was a lovely little thing, just like you to look at.'

'Perhaps if she hadn't been quite as lovely your son wouldn't have ruined her life by leaving her pregnant with his child,' she stormed at him.

He gave a sad sigh. 'Gregory was always wild, but—if I had known of your existence I would have acknowledged you years ago!' he rasped.

'Even an illegitimate heir is better than no heir at all?' she challenged contemptuously.

He suddenly looked old, not quite as tall, nor as arrogant. 'I probably deserved that,' he said heavily. 'Having a grandchild has meant everything to me in recent years, I've made no secret of that. I'd like to think that Gregory was deaf to my requests that he settle down and have children because he knew there was no reason for him to do so, that he always intended telling me about you some day.'

'You can live with your dreams if you want to,' Lise scorned. 'I happen to think that your son never thought of me again after writing that letter you were to receive after his death. And we both know by the date of that that he wrote it when I was three years old! Any duty he might have felt to me taken care of—and then forgotten!'

Gerald Farnham drew in a ragged breath. 'I can't pretend to have understood my son.' He shook his head sadly. 'All I do know is that you *are* my grandchild. And I'd like for us to get to know one another better.'

'I——'

'I never denied you, Elizabeth,' he cut in softly. 'I never would have done.'

'We'll never know that, will we?' she scoffed.

His mouth firmed determinedly. 'I understand that you hate Gregory; I'm not feeling too pleased with him myself at the moment,' he admitted softly. 'But,' he added firmly, 'we both know the truth now. I think we owe it to each other at least to get to know one another.'

Her eyes flashed. 'I don't owe you anything!'

He gave an impatient sigh at her defiance. 'Did your aunt or uncle ever give you a good spanking for being unreasonable?' He glared back at her, green sparks visible in his hazel-coloured eyes.

It suddenly occurred to Lise how ridiculous they must look standing beside a river glaring at each other, eyes locked, jaws set. It also occurred to her that there was more than a casual similarity between them, that this man was her grandfather, her own flesh and blood.

She had begun to cry then, held firmly in his arms, offering no resistance when he led her back to the road and helped her into his car, taking her back with him to Farnham Hall.

She had been here ever since, gently guided by her grandfather to be the sort of woman who was capable of running his estate. She had felt strange at first, like the village brat who had accidentally gatecrashed a life she didn't understand, or particularly want. But her grandfather had shown such pride in her, complimenting her effusively on each new accomplishment she made, until it had become the determination to *be* his granddaughter that had spurred her on to accept the new life he had provided for her.

After five years she was completely at home here, had *become* Elizabeth Farnham, Lise Morrison a part of her past that she remembered with affection but had no wish to return to.

She had almost forgotten she had ever known another life besides this one, even the expected arrival of Quinn Taylor back in her life not having disturbed her. She despised the man, saw no reason why she should explain that they had met before. And she had no intention of doing so!

Unfortunately for her grandfather, he seemed to have some sort of match-making idea in mind between her and the entertainer. She found it difficult even to be polite to the Canadian, didn't feel even a spark of that attraction towards him that had once made her so dizzily ecstatic. And her grandfather was going to realise that after he had tried to throw them together a couple of more times.

She moved to her bedroom window to gaze out at the west lawn, could clearly see the blue-suited figure as he moved about the stage. She had been wrong that night six years ago when she had supposed he was more at home in his casual clothes; he looked just as relaxed and comfortable in the formal suit.

The years had been kind to him, his attraction still devastating, in fact in some ways he seemed more attractive, his features ruggedly virile. His divorce several years ago had left him free to exploit that virility to its fullest, his name constantly linked with one woman or another. Elizabeth hoped he didn't waste his time by trying to impress *her*!

* * *

'I can't understand what all the fuss is about,' Giles muttered at her side.

Elizabeth gave a rueful grimace, longing to agree with him, but knowing it would be impolite to their guest of honour to do so.

Her grandfather had completely outwitted her in his effort to throw her into the company of Quinn Taylor, telling her he wanted this dinner party arranged at short notice, omitting to tell her that his guest of honour was going to be the singer.

The Canadian had only been to lunch the day before, and when no dinner invitation had been forthcoming she had heaved a sigh of gratitude. It wasn't until she descended the stairs earlier this evening to stand at her grandfather's side to greet their hastily invited guests that she had realised Quinn Taylor was going to be there. She had telephoned round herself and invited the dozen or so other guests, little guessing that her grandfather had personally issued one to Quinn Taylor.

She should have guessed really; as he had with her father before her, her grandfather had started complaining about his lack of great-grandchildren when she reached twenty-one. And he didn't approve of Giles as the father of those children, claimed he was too weak. She had never met a man yet who *was* as forceful as her grandfather, and certainly Quinn Taylor in no way matched *her* requirements of a husband!

She looked at him as he stood across the room from her and Giles, completely at ease in the midst of people she had found so overwhelming when she first came to live at the Hall. He was like a chameleon, had been equally comfortable at her aunt's and uncle's tiny farm all those years ago.

He wore the black evening-suit with ease, his skin very dark against his snowy white shirt, his dark hair curling slightly over the collar. Standing at his side was his partner for the evening, a beautiful redhead whom Elizabeth had instantly recognised as the star of a show she and Giles had gone to London to see several weeks before. For all his faults, he didn't seem to mind sharing the limelight with another star.

A polite mask shuttered her real feelings about him as he turned to catch her gaze upon him, smiling in polite ackowledgement of him before looking away again.

She might have been able to avoid him before dinner, but unfortunately he had been placed to her left at the long dining-table. Giles sat at her other side, and from the disparaging looks he kept giving the other man he was none too pleased with the seating arrangements.

She glanced down the length of the table to where her grandfather sat, knowing by the triumphant smile he gave her that he was deeply enjoying the situation. He could be an old devil, but she loved him, she acknowledged ruefully. The bond was all the stronger between them because they hadn't known of their true relationship for so many years.

But not even to please him could she be more than superficially polite to Quinn Taylor!

'Are your rehearsals going well, Mr Taylor?' she

turned to him with cool enquiry.

Those blue eyes seemed to be laughing at her as he met her gaze, as if he guessed at her ploy to get him to do what he hadn't done yesterday; talk about himself so much she didn't have to do more than murmur faint comments of admiration!

'Everything is going fine,' he dismissed. 'By the way,' he added softly, as if he sensed Giles's interest in their conversation. 'The perfume was a success.'

Elizabeth drew back abruptly, glancing at his dinner companion as she chatted huskily to the man sitting to her left. 'I'm glad Miss Barton approved,' she drawled.

He shook his head. 'Oh it wasn't for Maria,' he said softly.

No, she somehow hadn't thought it would be. The perfume she had been wearing yesterday had been light and slightly elusive, not at all suited to the sultry woman beside him who could lay claim to half Italian parentage.

'I'm glad—whoever, liked it,' she shrugged dismissively.

'Oh, she did,' he nodded, looking at her between partially closed lids.

She didn't have a self-conscious bone in her body, how could she have when her grandfather had paid tutors to come to the Hall to teach her how to walk gracefully, how to eat gracefully, how to make interesting conversation with even the most boring of guests, personally teaching her the runnings of the estate so that she could one day take over. And yet Quinn Taylor made her feel uncomfortable with the way he was looking at her.

Her hair had been loosely swept up on top of her head, her make-up was perfect, emphasising the colour and wide appeal of her eyes, her mouth a provocatively painted pout, the black gown she wore not revealing an inch of her creamy skin from neck to ankle, and yet she somehow felt exposed to this man's gaze.

'Giles, why don't you tell Mr Taylor about the horses you train and breed,' she heard herself prompt frantically, her anger rising at how out of character her behaviour was.

She despised this man, found him utterly contemptible; there was no reason for him to be able to unnerve her!

Giles looked surprised by her request too. 'I'm sure—Mr Taylor has no interest in horse-breeding,' he dismissed in a superior voice.

'On the contrary,' Quinn drawled—as if he were perfectly aware of the other man's condescension, and not in the least disturbed by it, 'it's something I've always wanted to do myself, but I'm afraid I'm away from home too often to be able to do it seriously. However I do have a couple of Arabians that I——'

Elizabeth withdrew with an inward groan; introduce the subject of Arabians to Giles and the rest of the evening would be taken up with it. She could also see a new grudging respect for the other man in his suddenly alert brown eyes, heaving an inward sigh as she realised she had probably just lost her only ally in disliking Quinn Taylor.

Colour darkened her cheeks as she met his laughing blue gaze, one brow arched mockingly. Damn it, she wouldn't put it past him to have found out just how boringly intense Giles could be on the subject of Arabian horses. Or for someone to have put him up to it . . .'

She glared down the table at her grandfather, her mouth tight as he gave an acknowledging inclination of his head. She could just hear him now, 'If Giles gets too uppity, just mention Arabians. The chap can go on for hours about Arabians!' Only Quinn hadn't even needed to introduce the subject himself; *she* had done it for him!

As she had known he would, Giles talked about his horse-breeding for the rest of the meal. And if Quinn Taylor was bored by the conversation it wasn't noticeable, his questions intelligent and knowledgeable on the subject. Perhaps he really did want to know—no, damn it, her grandfather had put him up to this.

By the time they left the table to have coffee in the drawing-room it was all she could do not to yawn publically instead of having to stifle the impulse. Almost two hours of Arabian horses as their main diet would have the same effect on anyone, she defended herself.

Quinn didn't seem to have been affected the same way; he was still deep in conversation with Giles as they sat drinking their coffee. For some unaccountable reason she felt as if Giles had betrayed her, gone over to the enemy. Which was ridiculous; he had merely found someone who appeared as interested in horse-breeding as he was.

'Something amiss, darling?' her grandfather drawled at her side.

She couldn't help smiling. 'Not at all,' she derided.

He arched iron-grey brows. 'No?'

Her smile deepened. 'I think it's wonderful that Giles has at last found someone who is as interested in horse-breeding as he is. The fact that I was completely bored through dinner isn't important,' she dismissed lightly.

Her grandfather frowned, as she had intended he should. 'I'm sure Quinn can talk about other things,' he defended hastily.

'Of course he can,' she comforted. 'And so can Giles,' she added sweetly.

He looked disgruntled. 'I've never heard him.'

She patted his hand. 'Probably because you've never listened.'

Her grandfather sighed. 'If you don't like Quinn Taylor why don't you just say so?'

Her mouth tightened. 'I don't like him,' she muttered intensely, all laughter gone.

'He seems to like you,' her grandfather frowned.

Elizabeth's mouth twisted. 'And Miss Barton. And the woman he purchased the perfume for,' she said drily. 'Really, Grandfather, I've heard enough about breeding lines the last couple of hours to last me for months,' she dismissed in a bored voice. 'I certainly don't need my own breeding potential discussed!'

He winced at her bluntness. 'I don't think there's

any need to be crude, darling,' he reproved.

'Don't you?' she mocked. 'Perhaps not,' she conceded. 'But I can assure you that marriage is the last thing on Mr Taylor's mind when he looks at a woman!'

'Did I ever say I wanted you to get married?' he frowned.

She looked up at him with wide eyes, barely reaching up to his shoulders. 'No, but——'

He shook his head. 'If you got married you would move away from here. I don't want that to happen,' he said determinedly.

'Grandfather,' she exclaimed disbelievingly. 'My birth was an accident; it certainly didn't set a precedent!'

'I'm sorry, darling.' He squeezed her hand in his much larger one. 'I've just never thought of your leaving here, to get married or otherwise.' He looked as if he were badly shaken that it could even be a possibility.

She gave a rueful shake of her head. 'Decided that great-grandchildren wouldn't be such a good idea after all?' she teased

'Oh, I still think they're a good idea,' he drawled. 'I'll just have to give my method of achieving them a little more thought!'

Elizabeth laughed softly; he looked deeply preoccupied as he walked away, visibly starting when one of his guests engaged him in conversation.

'Are you still angry with me?'

She turned sharply to face Quinn, her expression instantly guarded, frowning a little as she glanced across the room to see Giles in conversation with Maria Barton.

'He's telling her how wonderful she is,' Quinn supplied drily. 'It's something she never tires of hearing,' he drawled.

Elizabeth turned back to him coolly. 'I would imagine that applies to most people who choose entertainment as their profession,' she taunted.

'Touché.' He gave an acknowledging inclination of his head. 'I repeat, are you still angry with me?' he said softly.

She frowned at him slightly. 'About what?'

He shrugged broad shoulders. 'I haven't the least idea, but whatever it is, I apologise.' He held his hands up defensively.

He apologised so easily, and he didn't even know what he had done to make her hate him! At least he knew, he just wasn't aware that she knew of it too.

'You're mistaken, Mr Taylor,' she bit out coldly. 'I don't know you well enough to feel angry at you about anything.'

He sighed. 'You sure give a good impression of it.'

Her eyes glittered angrily. 'I'm sorry,' she snapped. 'How would you like me to behave?'

He looked at her consideringly. 'Maybe as if you didn't hate me quite so much,' he murmured slowly, his puzzlement obvious.

She gave a lightly dismissive laugh. 'Now you're being fanciful, Mr Taylor.'

'Am I?'

'I believe so,' she nodded coolly.

'Maybe.' He didn't sound convinced.

'Tell me, Mr Taylor, have you had the opportunity to see any of our Hampshire countryside?' She abruptly changed the subject, sure the last thing her grandfather would want was for her to insult his dinner-guest by telling him exactly why she disliked him so much.

He took his time about answering, obviously not pleased with the change of subject, and then he gave a barely perceptible shrug, as if he realised now wasn't the time or place for a confrontation—if there was to be one.

'Actually I've been in this area before,' he finally answered distractedly.

'Really?' she prompted disinterestedly.

'Mm,' Quinn nodded. 'In fact I'm rather pleased you brought the subject up,' he continued briskly.

'Oh?' A quick glance at Giles showed her he was still entranced by the actress, that he was going to be no help to her at all, when she so badly needed rescuing from a conversation she had no interest in continuing. And then something Quinn was saying caught—and held—her attention.

'—moved from the area, and the people that are there now said you might be able to help me,' he looked at her enquiringly.

'I'm sorry?' she said abruptly. 'I'm afraid I didn't hear you.' Her hands were tightly clasped together in front of her.

'I was just saying,' he repeated patiently. 'That some friends of mine used to live on one of the farms on this estate, and the people that have taken over from them said you might be able to tell me where they have gone.'

She could feel herself trembling, her body tense. 'Why should I know?' she shrugged.

Quinn frowned. 'Because they used to be tenants of the estate,' he repeated in a puzzled voice.

'Oh—oh yes,' she accepted jerkily. 'Perhaps if— you told me the name of the family?'

'Morrison,' he replied—as she had known he would!

Friends. He called her aunt and uncle his *friends*! How *dared* he do that when the next time they had seen him, after he had abused their hospitality by sleeping with their son's girlfriend under their roof, had been when he brought Fergus home to them in a wooden casket, dead at only twenty-three!

CHAPTER THREE

ELIZABETH looked at Quinn Taylor coldly. 'I believe the family moved to Portugal,' she bit out.

'Portugal,' he repeated softly, disappointment edging his voice.

'Yes,' she rasped. 'I believe they came into—some money, and decided to retire there.'

'I see,' he nodded slowly. 'A pity, I had hoped to see them.'

'If you'll excuse me,' she suddenly said abruptly, needing to get away, or she would scream. 'I have to go and check on something in the kitchen.'

She hurried away knowing her excuse was feeble; how could she have anything needing her attention in the kitchen when dinner had been over long ago! But she had needed to get away from Quinn Taylor, or she would have called him the murderer she believed him to be!

She almost ran out into the entrance-hall, knowing that several puzzled gazes had followed her, including that of her grandfather. But she had to get away, had to be alone, to think.

The morning-room offered her refuge, and she closed the door gratefully behind her, leaning back againt it weakly.

Poor Fergus, he had believed his dreams had more than come true six years ago when Quinn

Taylor invited him to go back to Canada with him when he left, so that the two of them might collaborate on some more songs, seeming to share an accord that had made that first song they did together an overnight success. Fergus had been ecstatic at the idea of going to Canada for a few months, hardly able to believe the break he had had.

And once again Terri had accompanied him, with the idea of possibly obtaining some modelling work there, she said. Lise had known the real reason the other girl wanted to go, knew it was so that she and Quinn Taylor could continue their affair with Fergus's presence as their shield. After all, Quinn Taylor was still married, and he didn't want his lily-white reputation tarnished.

And so Fergus and Terri had gone to Canada with the rest of Quinn's entourage. And six months later Fergus had been flown home to them in a coffin.

His letters had been full of enthusiasm for Canada and Quinn's home in the Rocky Mountains, their song-writing going well too. And then his letters started to arrive less frequently, and when he did write they would be hurriedly scribbled notes that didn't really tell them anything, except that he wasn't the same happy Fergus.

And then had come the telephone call in the night from Quinn Taylor as he told her aunt and uncle that Fergus had been killed in a climbing accident. A *climbing* accident! My God, what did Fergus know about climbing? Absolutely nothing! And if he had gone climbing it had to have been for a reason, something that had made him so unhappy he had needed to get away completely on his own. A reason like finding out he had been played for a fool, that Terri and the man he liked so much were merely using him to cover up their affair . . .

Terri had certainly only returned for the funeral before flying back to Canada, to complete 'work commitments', she said!

Aunt Madge and Uncle Hector had been stunned by their only child's death, even Aunt Madge's sharp tongue blunted as she withdrew into herself in her grief. Lise hadn't been able to stop crying, spending hour after hour in the music-room where she and Fergus had had such fun together, reliving all the good memories she had of the wonderful childhood they had shared, anger possessing her as those memories brought her back to that night six months before when she had realised what was going on between Terri and Quinn Taylor.

And then had come the self-condemnation. If she had told Fergus what was going on he wouldn't have gone to Canada in the first place, would still be at home with them all, still calling her Squirt in that affectionate way.

But instead he was dead, his body smashed and torn as he fell down the side of a mountain.

He had been flown home to them a week later, and to her horror Quinn Taylor had come back with him. Lise had taken one look at him and fled, staying away from him completely whenever he came to the house over the next few days as he helped her Uncle Hector with the funeral arrangements.

She had seen Quinn Taylor only once more after

that, across the width of Fergus's grave, and she had
hated him more than she had ever hated anything in
her life. He had seemed to flinch from her vehement
gaze, gathering himself to take a step towards her,
and then his attention had been drawn to Terri as
she sobbed at his side.

By the time he looked up again Lise had gone,
running away from the churchyard, and the man
whose presence she despised, as fast as she could go.

Life on the farm had never been the same after
that, as if Fergus's needless death had taken away
their reason for going on. Lise's work at college
suffered badly, and Uncle Hector no longer seemed
to have any interest in the work on the farm. What
would have happened to them all she had no idea,
because suddenly she was Elizabeth Farnham, heir
to the Farnham estate, and her aunt and uncle
received money from an unexpected quarter.

They were her aunt and uncle, the only parents
she had ever known, had cared for her and loved her
all her life, and with her sudden change of
circumstances she had looked forward to making
their life an easier one. But it hadn't been necessary;
the songs Fergus and Quinn Taylor had worked on
together were released on an album that instantly
leapt to the top of the charts when it was released,
the royalties that should have gone to Fergus now
paid to her aunt and uncle through his lawyer.

They hadn't known whether to accept it or not,
didn't really feel that it was their money. But Lise
had encouraged them to take it, to use it to buy the
villa in Portugal they had always dreamt of having

but never really thought to own. Reluctantly they had agreed, giving up their tenancy on the farm, somehow managing to leave all the unhappy memories behind them too. The letters she received from them were full of the new life they had acquired only because of their son's death. She had told them not to think of it in that way, knowing Fergus wouldn't have wanted them to feel that way about it.

Secretly she had always thought of it as Quinn Taylor's blood money!

If Fergus had never met Quinn Taylor he would still be alive today, she was sure of it. But instead he had been dead for over five years, only the happy memories left to the people that had loved him. And Quinn Taylor was here, in her home, daring to call her aunt and uncle his friends!

He hadn't been a friend to any of them, and she wasn't going to allow him close to her now—although she could tell that was what he wanted. No doubt he found it irksome that he hadn't been able to crook his finger and bring her running. Nothing he did would ever induce her even to like him!

It wasn't so surprising that he hadn't recognised her as Lise Morrison; the last five years had seen a lot of changes in her. The silver-blonde hair that had reached almost to the waist was styled in a straight bell to her shoulders, framing a face that no longer showed any signs of plumpness, revealing that she had high cheekbones within a heart-shaped face. Five years ago she hadn't even realised she had any bone-structure in her face! But the biggest difference of all was perhaps to her figure.

She was slender enough now to be a model herself. And with her new slenderness she seemed taller too, her legs long and silky, and not in the least chunky as they used to be.

No, Elizabeth Farnham bore little resemblance to Lise Morrison, but both of them utterly despised Quinn Taylor!

'Darling, what on earth are you doing in here?' Giles demanded in a puzzled voice.

She turned from where she stood staring out of the window in the darkened room, her emotions firmly under control as she gave Giles a warm smile. 'I didn't think you would miss me,' she teased, crossing the room to look up at him mockingly.

His cheeks flushed a little. 'I was only being polite to Miss Barton, if that's what you mean——'

She gave a teasing laugh. 'I know you were.' She put her hand in the crook of his arm, leading him firmly out of the room, too emotionally fraught to be alone with him where he might ask for more than conversation.

He sighed. 'Your grandfather wondered where you had got to,' he grimaced. 'He sent me to find you.'

She patted his arm understandingly, knowing how much of a bully her grandfather could be to people he knew were afraid to stand up to him. And Giles didn't realise that by meekly obeying her grandfather he was doing exactly what he didn't want to do: earning his contempt! She had tactfully tried to explain to him what her grandfather was doing but he couldn't see the logic behind her grandfather behaving in the way she described. *Logic* had nothing to do with the fact that her grandfather was a wicked old devil who liked to have his own way! If they didn't love each other so much they would argue endlessly.

As it was poor Giles was stuck in the middle of them, and it was becoming increasingly obvious he wasn't strong enough to withstand the pressure her grandfather would put on him if he so chose.

Her grandfather seemed to think Quinn Taylor was man enough; it was perhaps unfortunate that he had chosen the single man in the world she could never feel attracted to!

'And you've found me,' she told Giled encouragingly. 'Let's rejoin the party!'

She gave her grandfather a pert smile as he glowered across the room at her, launching herself into a mad whirl of talking to each and every one of their guests before it was time for them to leave; and Quinn was right about Maria Barton, she *did* like to hear how wonderful she was!

She carefully avoided any group of people Quinn himself might be talking to, deciding she had talked to him enough—relived enough harsh memories—for one night.

'Very well done,' her grandfather drawled at her side. 'It's almost not noticeable.'

She looked up at him blankly. 'What isn't?'

He shrugged, his eyes shrewdly assessing. 'Your avoidance of Quinn.'

'He's our guest of honour,' she dismissed without

so much as a visible flinch at her grandfather's continued astuteness where her attitude to Quinn was concerned. 'I've monopolised his attention enough for one evening.'

His eyes narrowed. 'Where did you disappear to earlier?'

'Really, Grandfather,' she chided mockingly. 'I surely don't have to account to you every time I leave to go to the bathroom!'

'Giles said he found you in the morning-room,' he challenged triumphantly. 'Just standing there in the dark.'

It was difficult to contain her irritation this time. 'I have a headache,' she snapped—knowing it was the truth. 'The darkness helped,' she returned the challenge.

'Then why didn't you just say so,' he said impatiently.

She sighed. 'Because I know how you worry.'

'I flap around you like an old mother hen with her chick,' he acknowledged ruefully. 'But you're all I've got, darling.'

'I know.' She squeezed his arm in complete understanding. 'Now let's go and say goodbye to our guests like dutiful hosts,' she encouraged.

He accepted her explanation, and she did in fact have a headache now. And it wasn't helped by the fact that she knew Quinn Taylor just stood looking at her as she made laughing comments to the guests as they left.

Did he see something of Lise Morrison in her after all, had he finally realised who she was? He didn't look like a man who had made a great discovery, just a man watching something that he badly wanted. And that he was determined to have!

She knew that look, had seen that same expression on her grandfather's face when he was about to argue for something he wanted. As he had argued about letting the Quinn Taylor concert take place here! She had put forward every reason she could as to why he shouldn't allow it to be given here, and for each of her arguments he had had an answer. But there was one argument *Quinn Taylor* could have no answer for concerning being attracted to her; he would never be able to overcome the obstacle of her hate and resentment!

'Elizabeth,' he stood in front of her now, taking her hand in his, his gaze richly appreciative as it rested on her. 'I can call you Elizabeth, I hope?' He arched mocking brows.

He was as aware of her listening grandfather at her side as she was, both of them knowing she would appear churlish and rude if she refused him the intimacy.

'Of course,' she bit out coldly, deliberately not calling him anything.

He gave a satisfied nod of his head before turning to her grandfather. 'You're sure about tomorrow?' he prompted huskily.

'Of course, dear boy,' her grandfather assured him effusively. 'We'll expect you around twelve.'

God, he had invited Quinn to lunch again! When she wished never to see this man again, three days in a row was a bit much. And she wasn't about to be manipulated by her grandfather into spending time with Quinn when she would rather not any longer, whether her refusal to do so made grandfather angry or not.

'I'm afraid you two gentlemen will have to excuse me from lunching with you tomorrow.' She gave them a bright meaningless smile that she knew hadn't fooled either of them for a moment. 'I promised Giles I'd spend the day with him helping out at the stables.'

'Mucking out?' Quinn Taylor mocked in a deceptively innocent voice.

'Certainly not,' a flushed Giles replied indignantly, giving her a puzzled look as he tried to remember when she had made him any such promise about tomorrow, both of them knowing that she and horses just didn't get on.

'Then perhaps she intends helping out with the breeding side of things,' Quinn Taylor drawled. 'Keeping the records straight, I meant, of course,' he added derisively as Elizabeth and Giles gasped simultaneously.

Elizabeth's mouth firmed as she saw her grandfather was enjoying the exchange immensely. 'I'm sure you couldn't have meant it in the insultingly familiar way you sounded, Mr Taylor,' she gave him a sweetly insincere smile.

'Did I sound familiar?' He raised innocent brows. 'I'm sorry, I didn't mean to be. I was just surprised at your arrangements for tomorrow when your grandfather told me the last time you and a horse actually met you ended up on your——'

'How positively amusing of my grandfather to entertain you with that story.' She shot the old devil a fierce glare as she spoke in her most haughtily condescending voice, mentally thanking the tutor who had assured her that tone would one day come in useful.

Trying to teach her to ride a horse had been the one thing she had persuaded her grandfather to give up on five years ago, her one attempt at staying on the back of one resulting in her landing rather painfully on a spot that made it difficult for her to sit down on anything for a week.

And how her grandfather had laughed when she told him Giles trained and bred horses for a living. But she had soon silenced him when she told him she only had to listen to Giles talking about his work, not actually participate in it.

But she should have known, considering the dismaying turn his plans concerning her and Quinn seemed to have taken since actually meeting the man, that he would take great pleasure in undermining her relationship with Giles to Quinn Taylor.

Quinn's lips twitched with suppressed laughter. 'I'm sure you didn't find it amusing at the time.'

'Why not?' she shrugged. 'Everyone else but the horse laughed. And I'm not so sure he didn't give a snicker too!'

Quinn Taylor grinned. 'I understand he tried to throw you off in the lily-pond first?'

She gave a haughty inclination of her head, mentally promising herself she would throttle her grandfather once they were alone. 'I suppose I should really have opted for the softer landing!'

'I've told you before, darling,' Giles reasoned indulgently. 'With horses it's just a question of showing them who's in charge——'

'Oh, Gulliver had no doubt about that—it was definitely him!' She grimaced at the memory of being perched precariously on the chestnut's back, the ground seeming very far away. When she had hit the ground with such a thump she had realised just *how* far. Since that time she had had no doubt that she preferred terra firma.

'That's because you——'

'You'll never make a horsewoman out of my granddaughter, Soper,' her grandfather cut in dismissively. 'So you might as well get used to that idea now.'

'I——'

'If we aren't leaving just yet I might as well have some more champagne,' the caustic voice of Maria Barton cut in, the beautiful woman obviously not liking it at all that she seemed to have been forgotten by all of them, most of all by the man who had brought her here. The two of them had hardly spent any time together during the evening. She looked at them all challengingly, her dark eyes flashing.

'We are leaving,' Quinn bit out, his displeasure crackling in the air. 'And I think you've had quite enough champagne,' he added tautly.

The actress flashed him the smile that had made her so famous, her beauty earthy and provocative. 'Can anyone ever have too much champagne?' she drawled huskily, draping her arm through his as she gazed up at him invitingly.

Elizabeth watched the display with distaste; Quinn Taylor seemed to be able to attract women like bees around honey—*all* women.

Except her, she dismissed. Only two more days until his concert was over and he returned to Canada; it shouldn't be too difficult to avoid him for that short time!

As Quinn and Maria were the last two guests to leave, besides Giles, they walked them out to the car, Elizabeth leaning into Giles as his arm encircled her waist as they watched the car depart. She moved away as soon as the car lights disappeared at the end of the driveway, giving Giles a bright smile as he looked hurt by her withdrawal.

'Give it up, darling,' her grandfather murmured softly as they strolled back into the house. 'The man has his sights set on you,' he enlarged as she gave him a questioning frown. 'And he seems a pretty determined sort of chap to me.' He smiled his enjoyment of the situation.

Her eyes flashed, and she shot a pointed look in Giles's direction before muttering back, 'Regaling him with charming little anecdotes about my youth isn't endearing him to me in the slightest,' she snapped.

He didn't look at all perturbed by her impatient anger. 'Well, I think I'll get off to bed now,' he announced so that Giles could hear too. 'Don't be long, Elizabeth,' he added mockingly. 'Soper,' he nodded abruptly to the other man.

Elizabeth watched him ruefully as he moved

lightly up the wide staircase. He was an old devil, showed his preference for Quinn Taylor quite shamelessly, but she couldn't help loving him.

Giles sighed at her side, also watching the older man. 'I wish I knew why he dislikes me so much,' he said woefully.

She gave him an encouraging smile as they slowly walked back into the drawing-room. 'He doesn't dislike you,' she dismissed lightly. 'He just enjoys the fact that he knows you won't risk offending him.' And did he take advantage of the fact!

'Why should I want to offend him?' Giles looked puzzled. 'I admire him very much.'

'Never mind, Giles,' she dismissed impatiently. 'It's getting rather late,' she added pointedly.

'Yes,' he accepted with a frown, moving to take her in his arms, at least a foot taller than her, naturally slender and elegant in his dark evening clothes. 'Did you mean it about coming over tomorrow?' he asked eagerly.

The thought of spending most of the day with the one animal that really made her nervous wasn't exactly appealing; but it was certainly preferable to having to see Quinn Taylor again!

'Of course I did.' She lightly touched his cheek, wondering why she hadn't been able to fall in love with this pleasantly attractive man during the three months they had been seeing each other. He was handsome, he was kind, always considerate, and yet the spark she had always expected to exist between her and the man she loved just wasn't there. She knew he cared for her, and she had hoped that with time—There was still time, she assured herself firmly, love didn't just happen in an instant. Or if it did, it was a love that was doomed to die when reality intruded, she told herself harshly. Better friendship and caring than an emotion that ripped the heart from your body!

'That's wonderful!' Giles beamed, lowering his head to capture her lips with his.

She could tell he was pleased by her impassioned response, the caress deepening after his initial surprise at her eagerness after months of only lukewarm passion.

She wanted that heady ecstasy she had known only once before in her life, slightly ashamed of herself as she realised she was using Giles, knowing he would believe she was at last coming to feel more for him than the easy friendship they had attained during the last few months.

She moved away from him awkwardly, evading his gaze after witnessing the heated passion in his suddenly dark brown eyes during the one glance she had given him. 'I think you had better go,' she encouraged huskily.

'Of course, darling.' He grinned his pleasure at her unexpected response. 'What time will you be over tomorrow?'

She stiltedly made the arrangements to see him at ten o'clock in the morning as they walked out to his car, giving a brief wave as he smiled at her warmly before driving away.

A frown marred her brow as she slowly walked back into the house, coming to an abrupt halt as she saw her grandfather watching her from the doorway to the library.

He was dressed ready for bed, his burgundy-coloured robe fastened over silk pyjamas. 'I couldn't sleep so I thought I would come down for a book.' He indicated the red leather-bound volume in his hand, eyeing her questioningly.

Elizabeth glanced at the drawing-room doorway that faced the library, knowing the door to the other room had been open all the time she and Giles had been alone in there, colour heating her cheeks as she realised the passionate scene her grandfather must have witnessed if he had been downstairs then.

'Darling, don't involve yourself in something you know isn't right for you.' He spoke gently as he realised she had guessed at his unintended observation of her and Giles together. 'Giles is a nice enough chap—for all that I mock him a little,' he admitted ruefully. 'I wouldn't want either of you to be hurt.'

He knew her too well, this man who had come to mean the whole world to her. She couldn't have loved him more than she already did if they had known each other all her life.

She gave a shaky smile. 'We won't be,' she assured him softly.

'Sure?' He looked concerned.

'Yes,' she said strongly. 'I was just—curious, for a moment. But don't worry, I'll let him down gently.' She sighed, realising that her behaviour tonight meant she would have to stop seeing Giles much sooner than she had intended, knowing that to do anything else would be unnecessarily cruel on her

part. She was very angry with herself at her
dishonesty, angrier still with Quinn Taylor, because
it had been the memory of the magic she had once
known in his arms that had caused her to seek the
same thing with Giles. The magic she had known
with Quinn all those years ago had been a fallacy, a
fantasy; reality was so much harsher.

'I know you will.' Her grandfather softly touched
her cheek, smiling encouragingly. 'You're a gentle
child.'

She didn't feel gentle as she stood at her bedroom
window gazing out at the shadowed image of the
stage that had been erected on the west lawn, she felt
violent, wanted to go out there and rip the structure
apart, wanted to rip the *man*, and what it had been
like to be in his arms, from her memory.

But somehow the images of Quinn remained . . .

Her day at the stables was not a success, as she had
known it wouldn't be. But she tried, she really did
try; could she help it if she panicked every time one
of the horses turned to look at her? Gulliver had
given her a look just like that before he reared up and
planted her painfully down on the ground on her
bottom.

It wasn't easy to keep Giles at a distance either
after last night, and she could tell he was hurt by her
avoidance of being alone with him. After the
encouragement she had given him the previous
evening he had probably been envisaging a long
romantic day *inside* the house, not having to witness
her making a complete hash of helping out in the

stables!

It was a long day, and her head ached by the time she finally took her leave, relieved that Giles was having dinner with one of the owners tonight instead of seeing her. All she wanted to do tonight was to soak in a long hot bath and then curl up in bed with her dinner on a tray. Just thinking about it made her groan with anticipation.

She somehow knew her plans weren't going to reach fruition when she entered the Hall just as a blonde-haired urchin came sliding down the banister of the wide staircase.

CHAPTER FOUR

ELIZABETH came to a halt in the doorway, staring up in amazement as a tiny figure dressed in tightly fitting denims that looked as if they had seen better days, a loose T-shirt that looked as if it would have fitted a burly rugby player, blonde hair steaming down her back, came flying down the banister with a whoop of delight.

The highly polished banister had tempted Elizabeth to do the same thing from the moment she had entered the Hall five years before, but because she knew her grandfather wouldn't have considered it in keeping with the ladylike demeanour he had always expected of her the temptation had never been given in to.

But whoever this young lady was who *had* given in to the temptation, she knew she had never seen her before!

The slender figure climbed agilely to the floor when she reached the bottom, giving the impression it was far from the first time she had done so.

A guilty blush darkened her face as she turned to see Elizabeth watching her, and Elizabeth found herself looking into the most delicately lovely face she had ever seen. Blue eyes twinkled beneath silky brows, the nose small and straight, the mouth a perfect bow above a small pointed chin. She guessed the girl to be in her early teens, breasts just beginning to thrust beneath the bulky T-shirt. Her hair was so fine and pale a blonde it looked almost silver, even lighter in colour than Elizabeth's own hair.

Whoever the girl was she had made herself very much at home. And Elizabeth was still certain she had never seen her before!.

'You must be Elizabeth, right?' the girl said ruefully, thrusting her hands into the back pockets of the tight and faded denims.

She nodded slowly, suddenly wary. 'That's right.'

'Sorry about the—the banister,' the girl grimaced, wrinkling her tiny nose up enchantingly. 'Dad would kill me if he knew I'd done it, let alone been caught at it.'

Dad. Elizabeth had a terrible feeling she knew exactly who 'Dad' was. But that still didn't explain what this girl was doing here.

'I promise no one will hear about it from me,' she dismissed. 'Now if you wouldn't mind, Miss——?'

'Taylor,' the girl supplied brightly. 'Marni Taylor. My Dad and I are staying here for a while.'

She had somehow guessed the girl might be Quinn's daughter as soon as she heard the accent. What she didn't understand, didn't *want* to understand, was the comment she had made about the two of them staying here. It couldn't be true—could it?

She gave a cool nod of her head. 'I'm pleased to meet you, Miss Taylor——'

'Oh, call me Marni,' she invited pertly. 'And can I call you Elizabeth? Or do you prefer Beth or Liz, something like that?'

After years of being known as Lise she still preferred hearing that as her name, but her grandfather had begun by calling her Elizabeth and somehow it had stuck; she had no intention of telling Quinn Taylor's daughter the only pet name she had ever had.

'Elizabeth will do fine.' She carefully closed the door behind her, walking forward into the entrace hall.

'This is a great house,' Marni told her with enthusiasm, looking up admiringly at the ornate ceiling above them. 'It must have been fun growing up here.'

She was surprised at the pain the remark caused, had believed herself over the bitter resentment she initially felt towards her father when she learnt that he had denied her her birthright. But it would have been fun growing up here, and perhaps she would never forget that she had been denied that because Gregory Farnham hadn't chosen to acknowledge her as his daughter. Strange, she hadn't thought about it for years. But then Quinn Taylor's presence here had brought back a lot of memories she would rather had remained forgotten.

'Yes,' she answered non-committally. 'Er—where is your father now?' She arched blonde brows.

'Rehearsing,' Marni supplied with a grimace. 'He's been at it for hours now. He always gets nervous before a show,' she shrugged.

Nervous? Quinn Taylor nervous? She didn't

believe he had ever known the uncertainty of the emotion!

'Then perhaps you can tell me where my grandfather is,' she asked politely, sensing his deviousness was behind the appearance of 'guests' she had had no knowledge of.

Marni shrugged again. 'I think he walked over to—the west lawn, is it?—a short time ago,' she concluded at Elizabeth's nod of confirmation. 'He seems to be a fan of Dad's,' she added lightly.

In more ways that one! No wonder her grandfather hadn't tried to discourage her from going to see Giles today; he had known damn well that she had more than lunch to avoid where Quinn Taylor was concerned. How *could* he have invited them to stay here without even telling her about it! All too easily, she acknowledged ruefully.

She gave an absent nod in answer to the statement. 'Is there just your father and you staying, or is Mr Simons here too?' She arched questioning brows.

'Bruce wouldn't feel comfortable staying here,' Marni dismissed affectionately. 'He stayed on at the hotel with the rest of the crew. But he's glad the problem of Dad's security has been solved,' she grinned. 'The hotel management were getting a little impatient with fans trying to sneak up to Dad's suite. Especially as they usually managed to get the wrong one,' she added with a chuckle. 'Only this morning an irate Arab complained about a young girl hiding in his closet!'

Elizabeth couldn't help returning the infectious

grin. 'It must have been a little—awkward for him.'

'Embarrassing, I think,' Marni said mischievously. 'Apparently he had just got out of the bath. And he was a little on the—plump side. If you know what I mean?' She pulled a face.

'I know what you mean.' She returned the other girl's smile. 'Doesn't it bother you that young girls chase after your father?' she asked curiously, firmly putting from her mind the fact that *she* had once been one of those 'young girls'.

'Not really,' Marni shrugged. 'It's all part of the image, isn't it?' she dismissed. 'And I know that Dad would never be interested in anyone of my age!'

'How old are you?' she queried calmly, blocking from her mind the memory of a time when she had believed he *was* attracted to a young girl.

'Fifteen,' Marni supplied, grimacing as Elizabeth couldn't hide her surprise. 'I know,' she sighed. 'I still look as if I'm only twelve years old!'

She gave the girl a sympathetic smile, having suffered being thought younger than her years most of her life too. 'I thought at least thirteen,' she teased lightly.

Marni grinned. 'I think you and I are going to be good friends.'

Elizabeth thought so too and, feeling as she did about Quinn, she knew that could make things rather awkward. She didn't want to see him as the family man, Marni's complete openness revealing just how much she loved her father, the fact that she was completely unaffected and unspoilt showing he was a good father to her. Marni wasn't going to understand the aversion *she* had to her father.

'I hope so,' she replied non-committally, regretful at the look of puzzled hurt in Marni's candid blue eyes. 'And now I'd better go and wash away the smell of the stables,' she added lightly. 'I'm sure we'll meet again at dinner.'

'Sure.' Marni nodded slowly. Elizabeth was able to feel her quizzical gaze on her all the way up the stairs to her room.

She hadn't meant to hurt the young girl, had genuinely liked her; it was the fact that she was *Quinn's* daughter that compelled her to be reserved.

Damn it, she hadn't thought of anything like this happening when the concert was arranged. She would just have to hope that Quinn's stay here was as brief as the one he had made at her aunt's and uncle's all those years ago!

That time he had only stayed overnight, an urgent call from London the next day taking him back to the city, and then back to Canada. Lise's relief had been immense, not knowing how she could even attempt to be polite to him after what she had witnessed in the bedroom next to hers. His hasty departure had made that unnecessary.

Being polite to him this time was going to be just as difficult, for all that Elizabeth Farnham was more sophisticated and self-confident!

But she knew her grandfather would never hear of asking a guest to leave, that, liking the other man as he did, he would probably find it difficult to believe in Quinn's behaviour with Terri and then Fergus's consequent death. She would probably have found it hard to believe herself if she hadn't personally witnessed his betrayal.

She really only had this evening to get through, the final rehearsal tomorrow afternoon, and then the concert in the evening. He would be leaving on Sunday. Surely she would get through one evening in his company?

'Is this the famous lily-pond?'

Elizabeth froze at the first sound of that huskily sensual voice, aware that it was even huskier tonight after the hours he had spent rehearsing. The loudspeakers had been switched on just as she got into the bath, and she had tried to shut her ears to the sound of his lyrically lovely voice as he sang a medley of those songs of his she had always liked so much. As she had lounged in the scented water the tears had begun to fall, the final song to fill the sunlit evening the one that he and Fergus had first collaborated on.

She had come down for dinner early, walking outside in the evening sunshine, knowing Quinn was now in one of the guest bedrooms, having heard him arrive home a short time ago.

He had lost no time in changing for dinner himself, she saw, as she slowly turned around to face him, his hair still damp from the shower he had obviously taken, very dark and attractive in the black evening suit and snowy white shirt. A chameleon, she decided again, able to adapt, with comfort, to any situation and background he happened to be in.

His blue gaze roamed over her appreciatively, her head back challengingly, knowing the green gown with its elusive silver threads suited her colouring perfectly. She was every inch the mistress of Farnham Hall as she coolly met his gaze.

'This is the estate's lily-pond, yes,' she confirmed distantly. 'Although I believe it just eluded being famous,' she added drily.

He grinned, completely at ease, although from the hours he had spent rehearsing he must be feeling tired. 'I believe you met Marni,' he drawled, standing beside her now as they gazed across the lily-topped pond that lay so still before them.

She gave him a sideways glance, wondering in what circumstances his daughter had told him they met. 'Yes, I saw her when I got home,' she answered non-committally.

'She won't be sliding down any more banisters,' he told her ruefully.

So Marni had told her father about the incident after all. Because she hadn't trusted *her* not to, or because the pair had such a close relationship Marni had been confident of her father's understanding? She had a feeling it was the latter.

'Did you enjoy your day at the stables?' Quinn asked at her silence.

She stiffened at his mockery. 'I didn't spend *all* my time in the stables,' she taunted softly.

Quinn rubbed his chin thoughtfully, the smoothness of his skin indicating he had taken his second shave of the day shortly before coming downstairs. 'Went for a gallop, did you?' he said innocently.

If this man weren't her grandfather's guest——!
'There are other, much more amusing entertainments, to be had at Giles's house,' she returned provocatively, her hands clenched at her sides, hating being the brunt of this man's amusement.

'Really?' he ground out, all amusement suddenly gone. 'Can't you find the same—entertainments, at home?'

She looked him coolly up and down. 'I can't say that I particularly *want* to,' she scorned haughtily, knowing he was offering himself as that entertainment.

'No?'

He was suddenly much too close, the air completely still around them, as if they were the only two people in the world.

Elizabeth wanted to resist as he took her into his arms, wanted to call him all the terrible things she believed him to be. But she was breathless, her resistance gone as he pulled her closer, a magic that stripped her of every ounce of strength and will-power that she had, completely taking over. A magic she had sought so desperately last night in Giles's arms . . .

She didn't need to seek any further, the magic had found her, her gaze held by his, her body moulded to his, her lips trembling slightly as she watched him lower his head towards her.

It began as a gently exploratory kiss, but as she leant weakly against him the caress deepened, becoming a demand, a command, for her uninhibited response.

Her arms were clasped about his neck as his hands slowly caressed the length of her spine, her shoulders, the rounded softness at the base of her spine, drawing her into him, his thighs as firm and hard as a rock, his arousal pressing against her.

She felt dizzy as her lips tingled from the light caress of his tongue, hearing a whimpering sound, and realising it was herself begging for more. Begging *Quinn Taylor* for more!

She wrenched away from him, breathing hard as she stared at him with self-disgust. She had kissed him, had wanted to go on kissing him. Oh God, how could she, how *could* she have wanted this man's lips on hers, his hands touching her!

'Elizabeth, it's OK.' He frowned his puzzlement as he read the vehemence of self-contempt in her eyes. 'We didn't do anything wrong,' he soothed. 'It isn't as if you're engaged to Giles Soper,' he encouraged as she still breathed raggedly.

Elizabeth's mouth twisted. 'Is that what it takes to stop you, Mr Taylor?' she rasped disgustedly. 'A ring on a woman's finger to show previous ownership!'

'No, of course not,' he said impatiently, still watching her frowningly. 'Your grandfather told me there's nothing serious between you and Soper, and I——'

'Maybe you should have asked *me* that,' she snapped with dislike.

He thrust his hands into his pockets, those long, sensitive hands that had caused such turmoil within her seconds ago. 'Is there?' His steady blue gaze compelled she answer truthfully.

She had never intended doing anything else! 'No, there isn't,' she bit out. 'But that doesn't mean I'm willing to fall into bed with the great star Quinn Taylor either!' she told him contemptuously.

He drew in a ragged breath, controlling his own anger with effort. 'We were just a man and woman enjoying each other, and you know it,' he rasped. 'If you want to tell yourself otherwise that's up to you,' he drawled coldly. 'But while you're deluding yourself, I'll know what really happened.'

'Nothing happened, Mr Taylor,' she said harshly. 'Nothing at all!'

'Elizabeth——'

'Excuse me,' she turned on her heel and walked away, trembling so badly she wasn't sure how she made it back into the house.

'Still pleasant out, is it?' her grandfather mocked as she entered the drawing-room through the open french doors she had left by earlier.

She gave him a fierce glare, daring him to say anything else. With a gently indrawn breath he wisely kept quiet.

She hadn't needed his mocking taunt to know he had seen her and Quinn together in the garden, had guessed that he had as soon as she entered the house. But if he tried to make anything of it he was going to be very sorry. Unwittingly it was Marni, a much more mature-looking Marni in a fitted knee-length dress of sky-blue, who goaded her further.

'Have you seen my father anywhere?' she queried lightly. 'He wasn't in his room when I went to call for him just now.'

Elizabeth swallowed hard, a flush darkening her cheeks at her grandfather's suddenly innocently questioning look. He would be well advised not to push her any more tonight!

She turned to Marni. 'He——'

'I was just taking a walk outside,' the man himself answered his daughter. 'And to answer your question, Gerald,' he drawled as he came further into the room, 'it's *very* pleasant out.'

Elizabeth's eyes widened at the challenge. What had happened between them hadn't been in the least *pleasant*, it had been—well, it had been—— She didn't want to think what it had been!

She was saved any further embarrassment on the subject as dinner was announced, although she deliberately broke etiquette by entering the dining-room with Marni, leaving the two men to follow behind them, knowing that she would otherwise have been forced to walk at Quinn's side.

'That's a beautiful dress you're wearing,' she complimented warmly, smiling as the other girl raised mischievous brows questioningly. 'It makes you look at least—oh, sixteen or so,' she added teasingly.

Marni grinned, her hair newly washed and gleaming almost silver down her spine, the very light make-up she wore adding to her maturity. 'Dad says I shouldn't be in too much of a hurry to grow up—or be thought grown up. But that's easy for him to say when he's old enough to have all the fun.'

It was impossible not to like this girl, her

friendliness was captivating. 'I bet he never even thought about sliding down the banister,' she drawled, and was rewarded by Marni's giggle.

'That's where you're wrong, Elizabeth,' he suddenly spoke softly behind them. 'As soon as I came into the house the other day I thought it must be a marvellous place for kids to grow up. Didn't you find it so?'

She turned to him sharply, searching the bland query of his face. Did he know? Had he somehow guessed . . .? No, of course he hadn't, he would have recognised her straight away if he had been going to do so.

'I really didn't spend that much time here as a child,' she answered evasively. In fact she had only been up to the Hall once when she was a child, and that had been when her uncle came up to see the estate manager about something, a time when she hadn't even got out of the car, let alone seen inside the beautiful mellow grey-stone house. Children from the village and surrounding farms didn't, as a rule, go inside Farnham Hall! 'Shall we begin dinner?' She indicated the small round table that had been prepared for the four of them in the comfort of the family dining-room rather than the larger and more formal room they had used for the dinner party last night and for the lunch with Quinn Taylor and his manager that first day. It was further evidence that her grandfather considered Quinn a friend as well as a guest.

She somehow managed to avoid further conversation with Quinn during the meal, although she was

aware of his gaze on her many times as she chatted
easily with Marni, her initial liking for the other girl
deepening as Marni showed herself interested in
many of the same things as she was. They both
dismissed the current fashions as unfeminine, and
their tastes in music were similar too, although
Quinn's music stayed firmly out of the discussion,
Marni too polite to bring it up, and Elizabeth
determined not to do so.

'Do you have the feeling we're slightly super-
fluous?' her grandfather finally drawled to Quinn.

The other man smiled. 'I had a feeling the two of
them would get on together,' he said.

And he didn't sound at all perturbed at the
prospect! 'In that case I take it you'll have no
objections if Marni would like to come shopping
with me tomorrow?' she prompted coolly.

'Really?' Marni pounced eagerly. 'That would be
great!' She turned to her father, her eyes glowing,
waiting for his answer.

Elizabeth wondered where the other girl's mother
was that the thought of going shopping with
another female should make her look so pleased. She
knew that Maggie Taylor had divorced her husband
several years ago, and it seemed that Marni must
have stayed with her father—unless she was just
with him for the summer holidays?—but surely she
saw her mother sometimes? Maybe Maggie Taylor
didn't like to shop, not all women did, although she
knew girls of Marni's age did. She, too, waited for
Quinn's answer.

Would he allow the fact that *they* had friction

between them to influence his answer? She couldn't believe he would be that petty, no matter how much her behaviour towards him irked him.

'Why not?' he shrugged. 'If Elizabeth is brave enough to face shopping with you I'm certainly grateful enough to miss the usual battle we have when you shop for clothes,' he drawled.

Elizabeth's brows rose; she was unable to picture him accompanying a teenager on a shopping-spree. But, being a chameleon, he probably adopted the role very easily. As he chose to adopt each new role as easily, including that of puzzled lover when she had rejected him before dinner!

Marni wrinkled her tiny nose at her father. 'You still think I have braces on my teeth—and should dress accordingly!'

'It wasn't so long ago that the braces came off, young lady,' he drawled.

'And boy, was I glad to get rid of those!' Marni grimaced with feeling.

'You couldn't go through life looking like Bugs Bunny, honey,' her father teased.

The cameraderie and affection between father and daughter was such an obvious thing it gave Elizabeth an ache in her heart. How could Quinn be this gentle with his daughter and yet have hurt a man who had liked and respected him so much his betrayal had destroyed him? She couldn't begin to understand this man—and she didn't want to.

She was deep in thought as they sat in the drawing-room drinking their coffee, giving a start of surprise as Quinn folded his long length down beside her. She was instantly on the defensive.

'No Giles tonight?' he prompted softly, her grandfather and Marni engaged in a conversation about the famous Calgary Stampede the young girl had recently attended.

'He had a business dinner to attend with the owner of one of the horses he trains,' she supplied stiltedly.

He drew in a ragged sigh at her distant manner. 'Elizabeth——'

'Darling, why don't you play something for us?' her grandfather prompted as Marni drifted off to look at the display of fans Elizabeth had collected in a cabinet.

She glanced awkwardly at Quinn; the last thing she wanted was to do anything that might jog his memory of her from the past. To do that might bring about her hurling accusations at him so ugly that she didn't even like to think about them.

'Not tonight, Grandfather,' she refused softly. 'I—I'm a little tired.'

'Oh,' he looked disappointed. 'She plays beautifully, Quinn,' he confided in the other man.

'I'm sure Mr Taylor isn't interested in the fact that I can manage to play a tune so that it is usually recognisable,' she dismissed.

'Darling, you're much better than that,' her grandfather reproved.

'I'd like to hear you play,' Quinn put in softly.

She shot him a resentful glare. 'I'm really not that good.'

'I'll even turn the music-sheet for you,' he

encouraged huskily.

'That won't be necessary,' she told him haughtily as she stood up to move to the grand piano that stood at the far end of the room.

She chose something light and fluffy, the theme tune from a Fred Astaire/Ginger Rogers film, knowing that although it was hardly a classical piece it was a tune her grandfather was particularly fond of. Both of them were addicted to the old black and white movies, especially ones that starred this engaging couple.

She faltered slightly as Quinn sat down beside her and played in unison with her, years of poised control coming to her rescue as she pulled herself together and resumed playing with her usual competence.

Time could have slipped back six years as they played the duet, in perfect accord, Quinn obviously familiar with the piece as he played without even glancing at the music in front of them.

But six years ago she had been a naïve young girl totally captivated by his magnetism and charisma, tonight she knew him for the selfish bastard he was.

Her fingers came crashing down on the keys. 'I really am rather tired,' she told her grandfather apologetically as he gave her a frowning look. 'I'll see you all tomorrow.' She kissed her grandfather on the cheek, giving Marni a strained smile, not meeting Quinn's gaze as she gave him a coolly dismissive nod before going to her room.

Oh God, she knew, she knew exactly what sort of man Quinn Taylor was, knew that if it weren't for him Fergus would still be alive today. But she also knew—had realised it earlier when she was in Quinn's arms, knowing it beyond a doubt as she was fully aware of him as they played the piano side by side—that the adolescent love for him, that she had believed had died the moment she found out about his duplicity, hadn't died at all. Despite all that he had done, she had continued to love Quinn Taylor all these years, *still* loved him!

The tears silently began to fall.

CHAPTER FIVE

ELIZABETH had debated calling off this shopping
trip with Marni with the excuse that she had a
headache, but she was glad now that she hadn't; the
other girl was full of enthusiasm, her company
stimulating and enjoyable. She didn't doubt that if
she had stayed at home this morning her grandfather would have tried to question her about what
he had witnessed in the garden last night between
her and Quinn. So far she had managed to avoid
being alone with him, not giving him the chance to
probe into yet another painful memory of Quinn
Taylor.

How a man so incredibly self-centred could be the
father of this enchantingly candid young girl was
beyond her. She could only assume that it was
Maggie Taylor's influence in Marni's early years
that had produced such a totally unaffected young
woman.

They had shopped until Marni declared herself
satisfied with her purchases, styled young enough
for her years, and yet hinting at the maturity that
was about to come. Marni had superb taste in
clothes, revealing that Quinn had only been teasing
his daughter the previous evening about the terrible
ordeal it was to take her shopping. She had even
taken the young girl's advice and bought several
things for herself that she might otherwise not have
bought.

They had lunch in a quiet restaurant away from the hubbub of the main street, both opting for a quiche salad, Marni tucking into hers with gusto.

'I'm still growing,' she excused herself as Elizabeth ate hers at a more leisurely pace. 'But not outwards, I hope.' She looked down critically at her slender figure.

Elizabeth thought of her own plump figure at that age. 'You look fine,' she assured. 'Have some more if you're still hungry.'

'Better not,' the other girl refused with a rueful smile. 'I don't want to be too late back, actually; Dad usually needs some moral support about now,' she revealed indulgently.

Elizabeth frowned. 'If he hates performing so much why does he put himself through it? I can't believe he needs the money,' she said, knowing Quinn was reputed to be worth several fortunes.

'Dad doesn't hate performing.' Marni sipped her juice. 'He just gets nervous beforehand; once he's out on stage he's as calm and confident as can be. And you're right about the money,' she grinned, sobering slowly. 'But he isn't personally making any money from this concert.'

Elizabeth frowned. 'I can't believe my grandfather struck such a hard bargain that he took your father's share of the profit too.'

'Oh, he didn't,' Marni dismissed smilingly. 'Dad does several concerts like this a year that go towards—Well, he has a pet project that the money from those goes to,' she explained with a shrug.

'Like a charity, you mean.' She still frowned.

'Something like that,' the other girl nodded.

No doubt his accountant had advised him it would be a good move tax-wise in the bracket he was in. And it didn't hurt his image any either!

'We had better be getting back, then,' she said stiltedly.

Marni gave her a puzzled look. 'I haven't done something to upset you, have I? If you still have doubts about the red dress——'

'I don't have any doubts left about the red dress,' she hastened to reassure her. 'In fact, I'm going to wear it tonight,' she encouraged, knowing how sensitive one could be at this age, realising her swings in moods must be puzzling Marni immensely. 'I just thought we should get back before your father becomes a nervous wreck without you!'

Marni's grin returned. 'You act as if you don't believe me,' she drawled as they left the restaurant after paying the bill. 'Have you ever thought what it must be like going out on to that stage to look at all those thousands of faces?' She gave a shiver. 'I couldn't do it.'

Neither could Elizabeth. 'But surely after all these years your father is used to it?'

'Dad has a theory,' Marni shrugged. 'The day he isn't nervous about being able to please all those people should be the day he stops trying.'

It made sense, and yet it was still difficult to picture Quinn as the nervous type. But then, she and Marni probably saw Quinn in a completely different way anyway.

The traffic was very heavy as they approached the Hall, people already arriving for the concert later tonight so that they could get a good view of the stage. Elizabeth waved acknowledgement of several of the estate workers as they took over directing the traffic into the appropriate fields for the day, several policemen already on the scene as they too helped.

'Looks as if it's going to be a big crowd,' Marni said excitedly.

'Yes,' she agreed tonelessly.

Quinn still wrote songs, and occasionally sang those by other people, although not very often, about love, and laughter, and sadness, songs that were completely attuned to people's emotions. She didn't know how he could express such lovely emotions when he was nothing but a selfish bastard who took what he wanted and damn the consequences!

She and Marni separated in the entrance-hall of the house, the younger girl taking her parcels and bags up to her room before joining Elizabeth and her grandfather for afternoon tea.

Her grandfather was alone as she entered the morning-room, and she inwardly stiffened as she saw his eyes begin to gleam satisfaction at having her alone at last.

She held up her hands defensively. 'Before you ask, nothing happened,' she drawled drily. 'Your guest kissed me, for a moment I kissed him back, and then I decided it wasn't what I wanted after all. End of incident,' she added firmly, sitting down in the chair opposite his.

'Are you talking about last night?' he queried lightly. 'Or is this some other time I didn't know about?'

'Very funny,' she sighed. 'There wouldn't even

have been *that* time if he hadn't taken me by surprise.'

'Caught you off balance, did he?' her grandfather mocked.

'Yes!' She glared at him, her eyes gleaming deeply green.

'Then perhaps he ought to make a habit of it,' her grandfather derided. 'For a few moments you caught fire in his arms!'

Elizabeth stood up restlessly. 'You're a wicked old man,' she accused heatedly.

He smiled, unperturbed. 'I know what I saw, Elizabeth.'

'Well, you won't see it again,' she snapped determinedly.

'No?'

She drew in an angry breath. 'Grandfather, don't—don't match-make between Quinn Taylor and me,' she said heavily. 'It's a waste of time, and I—it's embarrassing,' she compromised.

'You didn't kiss him as if you hated him, darling,' he pointed out gently.

'So he knows how to kiss like an expert,' she dismissed impatiently. 'He should do, he's had plenty of practice at it!'

'Darling, I think you're maligning the man——'

'And I think we should just drop this discussion,' she bit out tautly as she heard Marni's descent down the stairs, turning to smile at the young girl as she hesitantly joined them. 'Just in time for tea,' she greeted Marni warmly, the conversation between her grandfather and herself definitely over.

She had just finished pouring the tea when she

heard Petersham open the door to admit Quinn
Taylor and Bruce Simons. Her hands shook slightly
as she passed her grandfather his cup of tea,
knowing by his probing look that he hadn't missed
the way she had spilt some of the hot liquid into his
saucer.

She had dreaded this moment of having to face
Quinn again since realising that she was still as
much in love with him as she had been six years ago.

She kept her face averted as her grandfather
greeted the two men and Marni jumped up to hug
her father, remaining close to him with her arm
about his waist as she greeted Bruce Simons,
obviously treating the other man much like an
uncle.

Elizabeth knew she couldn't ignore the two men
indefinitely, and guarded herself against showing
any emotion as she turned to them with a politely
fixed smile. Quinn had obviously been working very
hard at his final rehearsal: his hair clung damply to
his forehead, the open-necked shirt he wore sticking
moistly to his chest and back. He looked flushed and
triumphant, although he frowned slightly as he met
her coolly dismissive gaze.

He oozed sexual vitality with that sheen of
perspiration still clinging to his brow, moisture
gleaming on the dark hair visible above his open
shirt.

She averted her gaze. 'Tea, gentlemen?' she
offered stiltedly.

Bruce Simons's expression at the offer would
have been funny if it hadn't been for the fact she
knew she would embarrass him terribly if she

showed by so much as a twitch of her lips that his
dismay at being offered *tea* was very amusing. He
looked as if she had made a mistake about his age and
offered him milk and biscuits!

'Or perhaps you would prefer coffee?' she added
with innocent query.

'Not for me, thanks,' Quinn refused softly. 'I
have to go and shower and change before I do
anything else.' He gave his manager an amused
glance. 'But I'm sure Bruce would love some coffee
and cakes,' he drawled.

The shorter man gave him a scowl. 'Yeah, I—I'd
love some,' he accepted without enthusiasm.

Elizabeth rang for the maid to bring the coffee,
having to repeat her request twice as poor Mary
gazed at Quinn with dreamy eyes.

'Perhaps you would like something brought up to
you in your room?' she suggested to Quinn once the
maid had left to get the coffee.

'I'm sure Mary would be only too pleased to bring
it to you,' her grandfather added drily.

She gave him a reproving glance; the poor girl
couldn't help her infatuation for Quinn. Unlike her,
who knew exactly what sort of man he was, and still
loved him in spite of that!

He had been watching her constantly since he
came into the house, unnerving her with that deep-
blue gaze that seemed to be able to read the secrets of
her soul. Why did he keep hounding her like this;
what did he want from her! Whatever it was she
couldn't give it to him.

'I think I'll pass.' Quinn drily refused her
grandfather's suggestion. 'Elizabeth . . .?'

She eyed him coldly. 'Yes, Mr Taylor?'

Anger flared briefly in those dazzling blue eyes at her insistence of formality between them. 'I'd like to talk to you before the concert tonight,' he told her softly.

This time she managed to clasp her hands together to stop them trembling. 'I can promise you that I didn't let Marni spend *all* your money,' she teased the smiling girl at his side, knowing while she looked at Marni that she didn't have to look at Quinn. 'We even left a few things in the shops for other people!'

Marni's grin widened. 'You should see the red dress I persuaded Elizabeth to buy for herself,' she enthused. 'It——'

'I thought your father wasn't interested in the buying of clothes?' she cut in sharply, not wanting the revealing style of the gown she had impulsively been talked into buying discussed with Quinn.

The other girl laughed softly. 'Any man with red blood in his veins would be interested in *that* dress!'

Dark brows rose over mockingly questioning eyes as Quinn looked at her curiously. 'Tell me more,' he murmured encouragingly to his daughter.

'Well, it's——'

'Thank you, Mary,' Elizabeth cut in firmly as the maid brought in the pot of coffee. 'Gentlemen,' she indicated they should take their seats while she poured them a drink.

'I think Elizabeth is keeping the dress as a surprise for dinner tonight,' Marni confided innocently.

Quinn's gaze slowly roamed over Elizabeth. 'I'll look forward to it,' he drawled softly.

That did make her sit up and look at him in return. 'But I thought you weren't eating with us tonight,' she reminded him a little desperately.

'I've moved dinner to six-thirty so that he can,' her grandfather put in cheerfully.

Her smile was weak to say the least. 'How lovely,' she muttered without enthusiasm, knowing by Quinn's self-satisfied grin that he knew exactly how she felt about spending more time than was necessary in his company. And she had believed, because of the time of the concert tonight, that dinner was one time she was to be spared the ordeal. Fate—and her grandfather—were not on her side!

She did her best to act the part of the gracious hostess once Quinn had gone up to his room to shower, but it wasn't easy when she knew her grandfather was watching her so closely. Maybe she should just tell him about Fergus and get him to stop all this, although no doubt he wouldn't be too pleased at the deception she had been carrying off the last few days.

She was still puzzling over her predicament later that evening as she dressed for dinner. In the red dress. To do anything else, just because she knew Quinn was going to be joining them after all, would be too obvious.

In the shop the dress had looked daring enough, but here in the privacy of her bedroom it looked like a dress that was begging someone—preferably some sexily virile man!—to take it off and feast on the beauty beneath!

Strapless, the dress was no more than a tube of material that clung to the slender curves of her body, seeming to remain in place over her breasts by pure magic alone. Her shoulders were bare, and the silky bell of her hair brushed sensually against her flesh, causing a tingle of awareness down her spine.

Giles, although he would love the dress and think, after the other evening, that she had bought it especially for him, wouldn't want her to be seen in public in such a gown. Very conservative in his outlook, he wouldn't appreciate the amount of flesh that remained bare for other men to ogle at. Now that she had seen the full effect herself she wasn't so sure she liked it either!

Maybe she could make some excuse for not wearing it, lie and claim that some of the stitching had come undone. Quinn would know it for a lie, but at this moment she wasn't sure she particularly cared what he thought, she was too vulnerable in the revealing gown. She——

She glanced frowningly across the room and then back at her reflection as a knock sounded on the door. It was probably just Marni, but she knew that once the other girl had seen her in the dress she wouldn't be able to change after all.

The knock sounded again, and she still debated about what to do. It would be rude of her not to answer the door, but if she did so Marni would see that she was obviously ready for dinner and expect her to go downstairs like this. It wasn't——

Her eyes opened wide as her bedroom door was gently opened and Quinn stood there looking at her with suddenly darkened eyes.

'I thought as you didn't answer that maybe you were still in the shower, or—or had already gone down to dinner,' he told her throatily as he stepped into the room and closed the door behind him. 'I see now why you delayed.'

Elizabeth's heart was beating so loudly she felt sure he must be able to hear it in the sudden stillness of the room. What was he doing here? He couldn't just walk into her room like this!

He was really too devastatingly attractive in the dark evening suit and white shirt, he seemed to make her bedroom look smaller, bringing the two of them closer together, something that made her very aware of the lack of material to her gown.

She swallowed hard. 'You do?' Her voice was husky in the silence.

He nodded his head. 'You can't go downstairs in that dress.'

She straightened. 'I can't?'

'No . . .' He shook his head again. 'Not unless you want me to shock everyone as I try to make love to you at the dinner table!'

She gave an irritated sigh. 'That routine might work with some women, Mr Taylor, but I——'

'It isn't a routine, Elizabeth,' he admitted shakily. 'I wish it were,' he added ruefully. 'I haven't shaken like this just looking at a woman since I was in college!'

'You aren't——' she broke off as he held up hands that obviously trembled. 'You're nervous because of the concert,' she dismissed. 'Marni told me you always——'

'Marni is right,' he bit out. 'But I don't shake when I'm nervous, I lapse into morose silence.'

She swallowed again. 'What do you want in here,

Mr Taylor?' Her sharp tone brooked no smart answers.

He let out a shaky sigh, unable to take his eyes off her. 'When I came in I wanted to talk to you, to try to solve the awkwardness there seems to be between us. Now . . .' he shrugged slowly. 'Now I just want to take that dress off you and make love to you!'

The heat that suddenly engulfed her body was a natural reaction to such a statement, she told herself defensively. Quinn had to know what he was doing, was no doubt as much an expert at verbal lovemaking as he was at the physical kind!

'I think you had better go,' she told him tightly.

'Yes.' He made no effort to leave the room.

'Now,' she bit out abruptly.

'Yes,' he said again, his chest moving shallowly up and down as he breathed raggedly.

'Quinn!' she prompted harshly.

The sexual tension suddenly became even stronger between them, a fire in Quinn's eyes as he moved across the room towards her. And she knew it was because, for the first time, she had called him by his first name.

'I've been longing for this since last night,' he murmured as he bent his head and claimed her mouth in a kiss that turned her body to molten silk.

She seemed to have been longing for it too, waiting, *needing* . . .!

There was no tenderness, no gentleness, just fierce passion that heated both of them, lips taking, devouring. Quinn's arms were like steel about her, his hands roaming restlessly up and down her body.

He didn't love her, she didn't love him in the way

that she should love a man who could make her feel this way, and yet at this moment it didn't seem to matter, nothing mattered but the moment. And the hunger ...

Mouths wide with desire, tongues duelling, hands searching, bodies seeking, finding momentary respite as Quinn pulled their thighs together, moving against her in slow erotic movements, the fire there becoming a burning ache throughout her whole body ...

She was burning in the hot sensuality, Quinn taking her mouth again and again, lips moist as they moved together hungrily. She arched her neck as those lips moved hotly down her throat to her bare shoulders, clinging to him to maintain her balance, gasping as one of his hands cupped beneath her breast, flicking the already hardened tip with his thumb-pad.

She fitted into the warm strength of his hand perfectly, as she had always known she would, his lips against the gentle swell of her breast above the red dress, sending tiny pin-pricks of pleasure up and down her spine.

Her breath came and went in ragged gasps, filled with a tension so strong she felt as if she might snap in half.

And then some of the tension eased as the naked tip of her breast was drawn into the warm haven of his mouth, the gentle suckling caress suddenly making the tension even more unbearable, wanting more, needing more, pressing Quinn against her as she begged for more.

The gentle caress became a pleasure-pain as he

drew on her fiercely, her gown pulled down completely to her waist as one of his hands cupped the other breast, flicking the sensitised tip in the same rhythm as he was sucking on the other nipple.

Her legs gave way weakly, and she fell back on to the bed, Quinn following her down, arching her spine so that she was offered up to him like a sacrifice, and he laved the other nipple with his tongue now, resisting all her efforts to increase the pressure of the caress, driving her wild with need.

A strong hand travelled the length of her thigh, teasing, tempting, searching, but never quite giving her what she needed.

'Touch me,' she pleaded against his lips. 'Oh God, Quinn, touch me!'

He looked down at her with fevered eyes, his hair falling carelessly across his forehead where her fingers had tangled in the silky thickness seconds earlier.

What he read in her eyes seemed to reassure him, and his mouth claimed hers again fiercely as he wrenched open the front of his shirt, material ripping as he did so, her bared breasts suddenly nestled against the hardness of his chest, the dark hair there an erotic abrasion against her sensitised flesh.

And then he touched her, as she had pleaded to be touched, his hand curved against her fiery warmth, the ache there becoming a blaze, tiny explosions beginning in her body as she felt herself about to lose control completely, breathing raggedly as time seemed to stand still and she felt herself on the edge of flight, of soaring as high as the stars—*higher*!

'Elizabeth?' a gentle knock on the door accompanied the query.

Marni!

Elizabeth didn't know who was the more shocked by the interruption, Quinn or herself, Quinn's expression one of stunned horror as he turned to look at the closed bedroom door.

She looked down at herself, at the red dress that had been pushed down to her waist to bare her breasts, dusky-rose peaks thrusting forward temptingly, her long legs bared too where Quinn had caressed her wildly seconds earlier. She looked like a wanton, could only guess at the tangled silkiness of her hair and her lips swollen with passion.

And Quinn's daughter stood on the other side of that closed door!

'Elizabeth?' she called again softly, obviously unsure of her presence in the room.

The two on the bed remained completely still, Elizabeth staring up at Quinn with pained eyes as his gaze remained fixed on the door. He was just as rumpled as she was, his bow-tie hanging loosely down his shirt front, his shirt actually ripped beside the buttons in a couple of places where he had been in such a hurry to know the feel of her naked breasts against him. His lips were as swollen as she knew hers must be, a fire still burning in his eyes. He looked nothing like the immaculately dressed man who had entered her bedroom a short time ago!

Dear God, if Marni hadn't interrupted them she had no doubt they would have taken their passion to its natural conclusion, that she would even now be in Quinn's arms as he possessed her completely!

Self-disgust ripped through her like a searing pain, and she felt ill at what she had almost allowed to happen—what she had actively encouraged to happen! God, how she had wanted Quinn, how she had *needed* him. The man who had been the cause of Fergus's death!

There was silence outside the room now, indicating that Marni had probably gone downstairs in search of her. Whether the young girl had gone or not, she couldn't lie here on the bed beside Quinn any longer!

She was pulling her dress back into place as he turned to her with dark eyes, scrambling off the side of the bed as he would have taken her in his arms, breathing agitatedly as the passion they had shared could still be felt in the room.

'Honey——'

'I think you had better go,' she rasped, turning away from the sight of him kneeling on her bed, the evidence of how she had raked her nails down his chest clearly revealed by the red welts on his flesh. Dear God, she had been so lost to passion she hadn't known what she was doing!

She swayed dizzily as she caught sight of her reflection in the full-length mirror across the room. Her hair was a tangled mess, her eyes still feverish, her mouth a swollen pout, completely bare of lipgloss but red and full anyway, the skin left bare above the red dress showed signs of faint red scratches, and she remembered how pleasurable the slight abrasion of Quinn's chin had felt against her as she burned for him. The dress itself was creased and still in slight disarray, and she was wearing only one of the matching red shoes, the other having fallen to the floor as she fell back upon the bed.

She looked like someone who walked the streets for a living, and she felt just as soiled!

'Darling, you——'

'Don't!' She turned on Quinn furiously as he would have reached out to her, her movements frantic as she moved to the wardbrobe to take out a different dress, any one, as long as it covered her from neck to toe. She would never be able to look at herself again without remembering Quinn's hands upon her!

The black gown was perfect. She would wear black forever, to remind her of how she had betrayed Fergus!

She picked up some sandals, holding them and the dress against her as she turned back to face Quinn. 'I said you should go!' She almost shouted in her agitation, her expression wild.

He shook his head, his face haggard, pain darkening his eyes. 'Not like this,' he refused gruffly. 'We have to talk. About what happened just now. About——'

'What *happened* was the great Quinn Taylor almost made another conquest by his *superb* love-making,' she scorned in self-disgust. 'I would be a fool to try to deny it, so I'm not even going to bother. But you were the one to come to my room, Quinn,' she bit out contemptuously. 'And I don't want you ever to do so again!' She was breathing hard in her distress, remembering all too vividly a time when *she* had been only too eager to go to *his* room—before she realised another woman had got

there before her! She had to go on remembering
that, mustn't ever let herself forget again how
selfishly this man took what he wanted.

'I came to talk, not to——' he broke off raggedly,
still looking pained. 'I want you, there's no denying
that,' he admitted heavily. 'But I didn't come in
here with the intention of making love to you.' He
sighed. 'There's already—so much tension between
us, I didn't want to add to that.'

'It isn't tension between us, it's *dislike*,' she
rasped harshly. 'I thought I had made that obvious
from the first.'

'You did,' he admitted heavily. 'I just——'

'Then why couldn't you have just accepted that
and left me alone?' she bit out contemptuously.

'Because that isn't *all* there is between us,' he said
quietly. 'There's also awareness, passion. And——'

'Awareness and passion,' she scorned. 'That may
be all you ask from your bed-partners, Quinn, but *I*
happen to be a little more selective. Usually.' She
looked at the rumpled bed with distaste. Her eyes
were bleak as she lifted her head proudly to meet his
gaze. 'Now get out of my bedroom,' she ordered
coldly.

He drew in a ragged breath. 'We still have to talk.'

'Mr Taylor,' she snapped harshly. 'After tomorrow, you will go out of my life, and I'll never have to
see you again. We have nothing we need to talk
about before that time, I can assure you.' She
dismissed him haughtily, turning on her heel to
enter the adjoining bathroom, knowing she was
going to need to shower again, at least to try to wash
off the feel of Quinn's lips and hands on her body.

'Lise . . .?'

She froze with her hand on the bathroom door, her breath caught in a harsh rasp in her throat.

'Lise,' Quinn softly repeated behind her.

Her back straightened, she forced herself to breathe again, turning the handle on the bathroom door with slow, deliberate movements, not acknowledging Quinn's use of her childhood name as she entered the adjoining room and locked the door behind her.

CHAPTER SIX

SHE was every inch Elizabeth Farnham as she presided over the dinner table, completely the gracious hostess as she even managed to draw Bruce Simons into the conversation, the poor man still slightly uncomfortable as he sat at the candlelit table being waited on by an assortment of servants.

Once again they were in the small family dining-room, the seating arrangement around the round table slightly off balance, with three men and only two women. But that lack of balance in their numbers had made it possible for her to seat herself between Bruce Simons and her grandfather, with Marni sitting on her grandfather's right, and Quinn seated between his daughter and manager.

After the deep shock he had given her in her bedroom by calling her Lise she hadn't wanted to come down for this dinner at all, had trembled as she waited in her bathroom for Quinn to leave her room, half expecting him to begin banging on the door she leant back against at any moment. But he hadn't done so, and seconds later she had heard the faint click of her bedroom door closing as he finally left, her tension leaving her as she sagged weakly against the door.

Obviously he had remembered her as Fergus's cousin, but when had he done so? That was what she wanted to know.

But not then! She was already too vulnerable at that moment to cope with any more trauma, needed to arm herself with her Elizabeth Farnham façade before facing him again.

And she had done so, not allowing herself to think as she showered and changed into the black dress and sandals, calmly standing before her mirror to retouch her make-up and brush her hair into its usual silvery-gold bell. The mirror reflected the image of a coolly composed Elizabeth Farnham, and it had been she who walked elegantly down the stairs to join the others for dinner.

She had only faltered slightly once, and that had been when Marni expressed her disappointment at her not wearing the red dress. She had used the excuse about some of the stitching coming undone, knowing she would never wear the dress again, her gaze unwillingly drawn to Quinn's shirt, knowing by the neat—unripped—appearance of the snowy white material that he had also needed to change before facing other people. The way she looked, and acted, now, she doubted anyone would believe she was the type of woman who would try to rip a man's clothes off him! And she would have done so, earlier, if Quinn hadn't anticipated her longing and bared his chest himself.

She had studiously avoided looking at him after that, either directly or indirectly, and he seemed to have lapsed into the morose silence that indicated his nerves about the concert had finally caught up with him.

Knowing he wasn't about to make a scene in front of the others—he would have done so before now if he were going to—she had relaxed slightly as she set about making Bruce Simons feel welcome and at ease. He seemed a little embarrassed by her undivided attention, but had slowly relaxed and almost seemed to be enjoying himself now.

Marni chatted brightly to her father, obviously not expecting any answers as she tried to encourage him to eat a little of the food that was placed so temptingly before him.

And Elizabeth's grandfather sat idly by and watched them all. She wasn't fooled for a moment by his bland expression, she knew him well enough to know that he sensed there was more to Quinn's silence and her diligence as a hostess than was obvious on the surface.

She couldn't help but feel an immense sense of relief when it was at last time for Quinn and Bruce to leave for the concert!

Giles was calling for her later and the two of them were going out somewhere to dance, far away from the chaos and noise that surrounded the Hall. She certainly had no wish to listen to any Quinn Taylor music, and it would be impossible not to do that if she stayed at the house.

'You aren't coming to listen to the concert?' Marni was scandalised, having talked Elizabeth's grandfather into accompanying her.

She shook her head thankfully, aware of Quinn's dark gaze on her. 'Giles—the man I'm dating at the moment,' she explained, remembering the other

girl had never met him, 'doesn't enjoy loud music.'
She gave a falsely regretful smile.

'What a pity.' Quinn spoke to her for the first
time since she had come down for dinner. 'I was
going to sing a song especially for you.' His eyes
were darkly compelling.

'Really?' Marni said, interested, her eyes glowing. 'Which one?'

Her father gave her a strained smile. 'It doesn't
matter now,' he dismissed softly. 'Enjoy your
evening, Miss Farnham,' he added harshly, his
gaze almost accusing.

She swallowed hard. 'I hope your evening is a
success too,' she returned stiltedly.

'We had better be going, Quinn,' Bruce prompted, waiting impatiently at the door.

'Yes,' he acknowledged, not giving Elizabeth
another glance as he followed the other man
outside, Marni hard on their heels.

Elizabeth couldn't meet her grandfather's gaze
as he stood in front of her, staring at the second
button down on his shirt, finally having to raise her
head and look him in the face as the silence between
them became unbearable.

He looked faintly reproving, and she was at once
on the defensive. 'I did warn you that Giles and I
wouldn't be attending tonight,' she reminded him.

He nodded slowly. 'That's your loss, of course,'
he drawled without rebuke. 'What are you running
away from, Elizabeth?' he added softly.

Her eyes widened before her expression became
guarded. 'I don't know what you mean,' she

dismissed lightly, deliberately evasive.

'You know,' her grandfather gently touched her cheek. 'It's what's making Quinn so damned miserable and you so bright and carefree you almost blinded me during dinner.'

'I was merely being polite to Mr Simons——'

'Darling, I may have had the pleasure of knowing you for only the last five years,' her grandfather rebuked. 'But during that time I've come to know you well enough to realise when you're upset. Something upset you very badly tonight,' he told her firmly. 'Uh uh,' he put silencing fingertips on her lips as she would have spoken. 'It's better not to say anything at all than to tell a lie,' he said. 'And you were just about to tell a whopper, my darling,' he chided gently. 'Don't worry, I'm not going to press you for the truth, I just want you to know that nothing is ever so bad you can't come to me and talk to me about it.'

She was too ashamed to tell anyone, even her grandfather, of the love she felt for a man who had been responsible for causing her cousin to be so unhappy he hadn't cared whether he lived or died!

'Thank you,' she accepted warmly, hugging him impulsively.

'But not yet, hmm?' He stroked her hair affectionately.

Tears glistened in her eyes as she looked up at him. 'I'm not sure I'll ever be able to talk about it,' she said raggedly.

'But it does concern Quinn?'

'They're waiting for you,' she said brightly as

he car horn sounded outside.

'Elizabeth——'

'Please, Grandfather,' she almost begged him, er voice breaking emotionally. 'Go and enjoy the oncert, and don't give me another thought,' she aid lightly.

He bent to kiss her fleetingly on the forehead. 'I ould never do that, darling,' he told her gently. But I'll wait for you to come to me,' he promised.

'And no more matchmaking between—Quinn nd me?' She stopped him at the door.

He looked at her searching, and she knew he ust be able to see the panic in her eyes. 'No more natchmaking,' he agreed slowly, his expression noughtful as he left the house.

Elizabeth closed her eyes as some of the strain of he last hour left her. She had known it was going to e difficult, but it had almost proved impossible vhen Quinn watched her so broodingly. But pride ad dictated she appear for dinner, and it had been nat same pride that had got her through the ordeal.

'Can I get you anything, Miss Elizabeth?' a oncerned Petersham broke into her tortuous houghts.

She turned with as bright smile as she realised he still stood in the entrance hall. 'No, thank you, 'etersham,' she said warmly. All the staff on the state had been wonderful to her from the moment he walked into the house as Elizabeth Farnham, 'etersham even relaxing some of his tight dignity s he explained to her she didn't call him *Mr* 'etersham. She had been brought up to believe it was polite to call all adults Mr or Mrs or Miss, and it had taken her a while to realise that Petersham found it hurtful if she called him by anything other than his surname. 'Could you bring Mr Soper into the drawing-room when he arrives?' she asked, going into the room to close the door behind her, needing complete privacy for a few minutes.

She couldn't help wondering what song Quinn had intended singing especially for her. which of his songs would have been most appropriate for her? 'Lying Lips', or 'Honeyed Kisses'; both of them told the tale of a woman who lied to the man who wanted her! Not that she had ever lied to Quinn, but he must believe she had.

God, she had nearly fainted when he called her Lise in that huskily pleading way! When had he realised who she was? From the beginning, yesterday, today; when? What real difference did it make *when* he had made the discovery? He knew now, and she wasn't about to deny it, or the truth she knew about him.

She had been standing at the window for some time, able to see the masses of people on the west lawn, when the music began to play, the crowd going wild as Quinn walked out on stage. As he began to sing 'Yesterday's Love' she could imagine him as he drew the audience to him with the charisma and warmth he exuded whenever he was up on a stage, each song telling a story, and every person in the audience drawn into that story as he sang of love and heartbreak and deceit.

'God, what a noise,' Giles said disgustedly as he

ame into the room.

Elizabeth instantly withdrew from the spell Quinn's singing had been wrapping around her, urning to smile at Giles, sure he wouldn't realise hat the smile hadn't quite reached her eyes.

'Isn't it,' she agreed with a dismissive laugh, crossing the room to accept his light kiss of greeting. 'Let's go somewhere madly exciting and orget all about the Quinn Taylor concert,' she ncouraged brightly, her arm through the crook of is as they left the house.

The club they went to was the most fashionable n London, full of the rich and famous as they all ppeared determined to have a good time, Elizaeth and Giles drawn into the mad whirl when they oined a group of several of their friends. They had un, they danced, they had a good time—and not nce, as Elizabeth smiled and flirted and laughed, id she forget about Quinn Taylor.

It was worse than it had been six years ago, now he had a woman's memories of him to haunt her ther than the calf-love of an adolescent. No matter ow much she hated him she loved him too, and as oon as he kissed or touched her that was all that vas important. She was disgusted with herself, ated her weakness, hated Quinn more for being nable to make her feel this way.

It was after two in the morning when they finally eft London, and she knew the concert would have een over hours ago. It would have been a success, f course; Quinn Taylor never gave less than his est in any performance.

He hadn't done any less when he made love t
her earlier either. But then that was just anothe
way of performing—with an audience of one
Maybe making love to her would have been a wa
of relieving some of his pre-concert tension!

She tersely refused when Giles asked if she woul
go home with him; she had done enough pretend
ing already tonight without adding *that* to her li
of mistakes.

'Not even for a little while?' he asked, crestfalle
at her refusal.

She shook her head. 'My grandfather is expect
ing me home tonight—no matter how late,' sh
added ruefully, knowing it was going to be afte
three when she eventually got in.

Giles looked disgruntled. 'If we were——'

'I really am rather tired,' she excused herse
hastily; the last thing she wanted tonight was
proposal from Giles! She liked him, she liked him
lot, but soon, very soon if he continued to act in th
possessive way, she was going to have to tell hir
she wouldn't be seeing him any more. She had bee
putting it off until after Quinn had left so that n
mistake was made about her motives for not seein
Giles any more.

'All right.' Giles accepted her refusal though h
was disappointed. 'Tomorrow?'

She and her grandfather would have the hous
back to themselves then, and she was sure he
grandfather would give her the privacy to talk t
Giles alone. 'I'll call you,' she nodded, regretful
having to hurt this man, but knowing, now mor

han ever, that she could never feel anything but
liking for him. How ironic: she liked Giles but
could never love him, and she loved Quinn but
could never like him! Once she had purged Quinn
from her heart she hoped there would be a man she
could both like *and* love.

The Hall was very silent as she let herself into the
house, the servants having gone to bed long ago, as
had her grandfather and their guests. Why not, it
was almost morning now!

'Hello, Lise.'

She turned sharply, facing Quinn as he stood in
the library doorway, nursing a glass of what
looked like whisky in his hand, looking tired and
strained, casually dressed in an open-necked blue
shirt and faded denims. Obviously not *all* of their
guests had gone to bed after all.

She forced herself to be calm, raising a haughty
brow at him questioningly. 'That's the third time
this evening you've called me by that name,' she
drawled as she walked across the hallway, looking
at him pointedly as she waited for him to move
aside and let her into the room. He had obviously
been sitting in one of the wide-backed leather
chairs that stood either side of the unlit fireplace, a
book lying open on the small table beside it. She
turned confidently to face him. 'An old girlfriend?'
she drawled mockingly.

He gave a deep sigh, closing the door softly
behind him, staring down at the contents of the
glass in his hand for several minutes. 'She was a
girl, yes,' he spoke huskily, the two-hour concert

obviously having put severe strain on his voice. '
had hoped she was a friend.' He watched he
closely. 'But something went wrong between us.

'What a pity,' she dismissed insincerely, havin
received a jolt as he fell in with her game. Wh
didn't he just say that he knew exactly who she wa
and get it over with! Or maybe he still wasn't sure
Although she found that hard to believe after he
reaction earlier tonight when he called her Lise
'Did the concert go well?' she asked politely.

He looked irritated by the change of subject
'Bruce said it did,' he dismissed tersely.

'Don't you think it did?' she cautioned, sittin
down in the chair opposite the one he ha
occupied, dropping her clutch-bag down on to th
small leather-topped table that stood beside it.

Her grandfather didn't have a study, claimed h
couldn't bear rooms that resembled offices, and s
the library was the closest he came to having a roon
in the house he worked in. Its lived-in appearanc
was evidence that he spent a lot of time in here, an
often during cold winter evenings Elizabeth woul
curl up in this very same chair beside a roaring fir
and keep him company while he worked.

Quinn shrugged in answer to her question. 'T
tell you the truth I didn't particularly care abou
anything else after the way we parted earlier thi
evening,' he rasped, his eyes bleak.

Inwardly she stiffened, but outwardly sh
remained coolly composed. 'I have no doubt I'll se
the concert when it appears on television,' sh
shrugged, implying she would then judge fo

herself whether it had been good or not.

Quinn watched her broodingly, making Elizabeth shift uncomfortably in spite of herself. 'Where the hell have you been all evening?' he suddenly rasped. 'Or should I say night?' he added harshly.

Her eyes widened at the attack. 'I don't believe I have to tell you that, Mr Taylor——'

'Will you drop this Mr Taylor garbage!' he bit out tautly, putting his glass down to thrust his hands into his denims pockets, the whisky obviously not his first of the evening if his mood was anything to go by.

'If you insist—Quinn,' she amended carelessly. 'I really shouldn't worry about the concert, Quinn, I'm sure it was excellent. No doubt my grandfather will want to see it when it comes on television, so I——'

'Will you just forget about the concert!' he exploded fiercely. 'I'm not interested in the damn thing now that it's over. What I *am* interested in is what happened to that girl Lise I once knew?' he probed almost gently, his gaze intent.

She gave a casual shrug of her shoulders. 'I would say it's a certainty that she grew up.'

His eyes narrowed, his mouth a taut line. 'And became Elizabeth Farnham.'

'Oh I'm sure it wasn't quite as easy as that,' she lightly dismissed. 'But I doubt whether I'm the first illegitimate child the local "lord of the manor" has left on some poor unsophisticated girl who believed herself in love with him!' she scorned.

'Is that what happened?' Quinn prompted softly.

Her eyes flashed. 'Exactly,' she bit out. 'He refused to marry her, of course,' she said. 'My mother died giving birth to me, and Gregory Farnham went merrily on with his life—although there were no more little bastards left littering up the countryside that we know of!' she said with contempt.

'But he must have finally acknowledged you if——'

'In a letter to be read after he was dead,' she revealed hardly. 'He died five years ago,' she dismissed abruptly.

'Dear God,' Quinn shook his head disbelievingly. 'How could he have done that to you?'

Her grandfather was the only one that had ever understood how betrayed she had felt by her father, everyone else, including her aunt and uncle, thought she should be thankful that she was the heiress, Elizabeth Farnham, no matter how many years it had taken for her to be acknowledged as such. She didn't appreciate Quinn being able to understand how she felt too.

'It isn't important,' she lied. 'I am Elizabeth Farnham now, no matter how it happened.'

'You said we had never met before,' he reminded her tensely.

'I *said* I'm sure I would remember if we had met before,' she corrected, looking at him coldly. 'I remember it very well. I just had no wish to pursue the acquaintance.'

'And left me wondering where the hell I knew you from,' he rasped harshly.

'I don't suppose it took up too much of your time,' she drawled derisively. 'When *did* you realise who I was, the night my grandfather persuaded me to play the piano for you all?'

He shook his head. 'I knew the moment I kissed Elizabeth Farnham for the first time.'

She stiffened. 'Don't tell me you remember all the women you've kissed?' she scorned harshly.

He drew in a harsh breath. 'There really haven't been that many. Have you forgotten I was married for ten years?'

'Did you?' she mocked contemptuously.

His eyes narrowed as he stared down at her tensely. 'If you're asking if I was ever unfaithful during my marriage the answer is no!'

'Really?' she returned disbelievingly. 'But you remember kissing a seventeen-year-old girl in her uncle's cowshed?' she scoffed disgustedly.

'I remember,' he spoke slowly, softly. 'Kissing her because she asked me to. And then I remember kissing her again because I hurt her by ending the first kiss when it became much more than a birthday gift for a girl almost young enough to be my own daughter!' He looked bleak. 'I'm not sure when—or if—the second kiss would have ended if Fergus and Terri hadn't interrupted us,' he admitted raggedly.

'Oh come on, Quinn,' Elizabeth dismissed scornfully. 'I was an infatuated child, and you wanted a woman to warm your bed that night.'

He became suddenly still, his eyes narrowed. 'What the hell are you talking about?'

She stood up. 'I'm tired, Quinn,' she bit out coldly. 'I'd like to go to bed now.

He grasped her arm as she would have walked past him. 'You can't make a statement like that and just walk out on me,' he grated, his eyes fierce.

She met his gaze unflinchingly. 'Can't I?' she taunted. 'This is my home, Mr Taylor,' she reminded coldly. 'I believe I can do what I like in it!' She looked down pointedly at his hand still holding her arm as he restrained her from walking away.

'Does that include insulting one of your grand-father's guests——'

'I'm not insulting you.' She wrenched out of his grasp, uncaring of the bruises she had probably inflicted on her own flesh. 'Believe me,' she laughed without humour, 'if I once began insulting you I wouldn't know where to stop!' She looked at him with glacial eyes, not wanting to begin hurling those accusations at him, knowing she *wouldn't* know how to stop once she started, all her hatred and disgust bubbling to the surface to spill over in a vitriolic attack that might leave him in no doubt of her dislike of him but would also leave her shattered and broken. 'I think it's best if we end this conversation right here,' she told him coldly, walking towards the door.

'Lise, I want to know what you meant just now about a woman in my bed?' he prompted harshly.

She spun around. 'Don't call me that name,' she

demanded harshly. 'Don't ever call me that again!'

'OK.' He held up his hands defensively. 'For the moment I'll——'

'I said don't *ever* call me by that name!' she repeated fiercely, her eyes shooting tiny gold flames amongst the green. 'You don't have the right!'

He became suddenly still. 'Why don't I?'

She faced him tensely across the room. 'Don't make me say it,' she began to tremble.

Quinn's eyes narrowed. 'Say what?' he encouraged softly.

She drew in a ragged breath, could feel her control slipping, knowing she couldn't contain her heated dislike any longer, wanting to escape before it flamed out of control.

Her eyes flared indignantly, furiously, her hands clenched at her sides. 'You have no right to use that name because it was Fergus's name for me.' She spat the words at him. 'And because we both know *you're* the reason he died, you and Terri, with your affair that you thought no one knew about but which *I* witnessed, to my disgust, and which Fergus obviously found out about before he went *climbing*!' She wrenched open the door, running from the room.

CHAPTER SEVEN

QUINN caught up with her at the bottom of the stairs, clasping her arm to spin her back round to face him. 'You can't make an accusation like that and just walk away from it!' he rasped, his eyes dark with anger.

She gave a choked sob of a laugh. 'I wasn't walking; I was running!' She tried to shake off his hold on her arm, her breathing agitated as he refused to let her go. 'Let me go, Quinn,' she ordered shakily. 'Before I say anything else to make our situation here impossible.'

He let her go, but his gaze compelled her to stay where she was. 'I don't think it could be any more impossible,' he muttered self-derisively. 'You believe,' he said slowly. 'that I—metaphorically— pushed Fergus to his death five years ago? He prompted harshly, 'At least, I hope that accusation was meant metaphorically.' He looked at her with narrowed eyes.

Her mouth twisted. 'I don't think you're the type actually to push a man off a mountain, if that's what you mean,' she rasped. 'But I know how much Fergus loved Terri. And I also know the two of you were having an affair,' she added contemptuously.

Quinn shook his head in puzzlement. 'How do you know that?'

Her eyes became glacial once again. 'That night you stayed with us Terri was supposed to be sharing my room. Yes,' she scorned as comprehension darkened his eyes. 'On my way—on my way to the bathroom,' she invented, determined not to admit to the depths of her own infatuation six years ago, the intensity of those feelings driving her to seek out Quinn in his bedroom, 'I heard the two of you together in your bedroom.' Her expression was full of disgust. 'She didn't return to my bedroom until early the next morning,' Elizabeth added contemptuously. 'I was pretty innocent at seventeen,' she said self-derisively. 'But even I could tell that Terri had the look of a woman who had been making love most of the night!'

Quinn turned away, his shoulders hunched over as his hands were thrust into his trouser pockets. He drew in a ragged breath, his eyes dark when he turned to face her. 'Aren't you assuming a lot believing I was the one she had been making love with?' he finally questioned, his eyes narrowed.

'From what I overheard,' said Elizabeth, 'it was far from the first time it had happened! Besides, you looked pretty haggard yourself when you came down to breakfast the next morning.' She could vividly recall how she had avoided looking at him after that first probing glance, the lines of tiredness about his eyes evidence of his own sleepless night.

He sighed. 'Maybe I did,' he nodded. 'But it had nothing to do with Terri. Obviously I can't say for certain, but I would say it's pretty obvious she spent the rest of the night in Fergus's room—because she certainly didn't spend it in mine!' he concluded hardly.

'No?' Elizabeth said without conviction.

'No,' he scowled at her. 'Lise—Elizabeth,' he hastily amended as her eyes flashed fiercely once again. 'I didn't have an affair with Terri, not then, nor later in Canada. Maybe it's asking a lot for you to believe that, but——'

'It's asking the impossible,' she dismissed hardly. 'I *heard* the two of you together that night,' she reminded him with distaste. 'I also read Fergus's letters from Canada as he seemed to become more and more disillusioned with what was going on out there. He was obviously deeply unhappy before— before he died.'

'And you believe that was because I was having an affair with his girlfriend,' Quinn rasped.

'Yes,' she bit out abruptly.

His breath raggedly left his body. '*That's* why you looked at me with such hate across Fergus's grave.'

'Should I have looked at you with love?' she scorned. 'A man who saw something he wanted and took it, regardless of the fact that it was the girlfriend of a man who liked and respected you? I just thank God my aunt and uncle never knew what really happened, because if they had they would never have accepted the money your recording company paid them on Fergus's behalf. And that was a small price for you to have to pay for ruining their son's life so that he had no reason to go on living!'

Quinn drew in a harshly controlling breath. 'I

think you were right, this conversation should have ended ten minutes ago,' he rasped. 'We can talk again when you're—calmer.'

'I'll never be calm enough to listen as you try to excuse what you did to Fergus,' she scorned. 'Oh, I always knew Terri wasn't good enough for him, that she just liked the idea of having a song-writer for a boyfriend, that it fitted in with that glamorous life she portrayed for herself. But Fergus believed you were his friend, and you betrayed him!'

'I may have unwittingly—and unwillingly— contributed to Fergus's death,' he admitted harshly. 'But I would like to explain that without heat or anger——'

'Please don't bother to try to explain how you could be so obsessed with a woman like Terri that friendship and trust were completely forgotten,' she dismissed with contempt. 'I'm not interested in hearing that sort of explanation.' She turned away wearily. He had admitted it, had acknowledged that he had helped push Fergus—metaphorically—to his death! Somehow she had always hoped—especially after discovering that she still loved him!—that he could explain away his involvement with Terri, assure her that it had had nothing to do with Fergus's death. There was no hope left after Quinn's confession.

'You will be interested, Lise,' Quinn's voice warned her as she went up the stairs. 'We both know that there's something between us far stronger than what you *believe* happened, that even though you think you hate me, you want me too.'

She kept walking, her back rigid, knowing he watched her but refusing to look at him again.

The tears held off until she reached the sanctuary of her bedroom, and then they cascaded down her cheeks, her body racked by heartbreaking sobs.

She had said them, all the ugly accusations that she had lived with the last six years. And Quinn hadn't been able to deny the ones that really mattered.

'—invited them to stay on for a while,' her grandfather concluded, looking at her intently as it became obvious she hadn't heard a word he had said. 'Darling, what is wrong with you today?' He frowned at her worriedly. 'You were very late home last night; did something happen that I should know about?'

They were seated at the breakfast table, both of them down early this morning. Elizabeth knew her grandfather always ate early, and as she hadn't even attempted to go to bed herself she had decided to join him, ignoring the platters of food to sip at a cup of strong sweetened coffee.

She smiled wanly at her grandfather's method of asking if Giles had behaved himself the evening before. 'Nothing at all,' she dismissed. 'I was late home because Giles and I met several friends at the club. Now what were you saying . . .?' She made a concerted effort to concentrate on what he was saying.

He nodded, although he still frowned at her concernedly. 'Quinn doesn't have any reason to rush back to Alberta, so I've invited him and Marni to stay on for a while now that the concert is over,' he revealed briskly, sitting forward worriedly as she instantly paled. 'Darling, are you sure you're all right?' he frowned.

He had invited Quinn to stay on. But he couldn't stay, wouldn't want to stay, after their conversation last night!

Some of the colour returned to her cheeks. 'Fine,' she dismissed brightly. 'Late evenings don't agree with me, I guess,' she shrugged, attempting to smile. 'So you've invited Mr Taylor to stay on,' she repeated abruptly.

'Yes,' Her grandfather still watched her closely. 'That isn't going to be a problem for you, is it, darling?'

No, because she was sure Quinn wouldn't *be* staying on! 'He's your guest, Grandfather.' She smiled.

'Yes,' he sighed. 'But you haven't seemed quite yourself since he arrived. Maybe inviting him to stay on wasn't such a good idea,' he accepted, 'but he looked so tired this morning that I thought the rest might do him good. He ——'

'This morning?' Elizabeth echoed sharply. 'You made this invitation this morning?'

He nodded. 'Quinn was up at the crack of dawn, taking me up on my offer of an early morning ride. He should be back any moment for his breakfast; he wasn't hungry earlier.'

She had imagined Quinn was still in bed, not off riding on the estate somewhere. She had found it impossible to sleep after leaving him last night, hadn't even bothered to go to bed; from the earliness of the hour when he and her grandfather had spoken she could only presume he had spent a restless night too. Maybe a guilty conscience did that to you!

She sipped her coffee. 'Don't be too disappointed if he turns down your invitation,' she advised gently. 'After all, he's a busy man, and——'

'But he's already accepted,' her grandfather cut in lightly. 'Thanked me very much and said he would be delighted. Or something like that,' he grimaced.

Quinn couldn't stay on here, couldn't want to, not now. Then why had he accepted the invitation? What did he hope to prove? Didn't he realise that she hated him, that it could only prove awkward for both of them if he chose to remain here?

He had to know all those things, but perhaps he considered them all unimportant compared to the fact that they desired each other!

Oh God, how was she to get through the rest of his visit? It had seemed bad enough when she only had until today to get through, but even so she hadn't managed it without telling him exactly how contemptible she found him; how much longer did he intend staying on here?

'Er—how long did you make this invitation for?' she asked her grandfather casually.

'I didn't specify a time,' he shrugged. 'I suppose it will be until he has other commitments that take him away.'

Considering the fact that Quinn had done less and less public performing in recent years, that could be a matter of weeks rather than days!

'He said he's in no hurry to get back.' Her grandfather confirmed her suspicion. 'To tell you the truth, I think he rather likes this part of England,' he added smugly.

Elizabeth bitterly wondered if he had bothered to visit the local churchyard during his stay here. She regularly placed flowers on Fergus's grave there, knowing that it comforted her aunt and uncle to know that she did so. She doubted if Quinn had given the grave there another thought since the funeral five and a half years ago.

'That's nice,' she said non-committally. 'Grandfather, would you—would you mind if I went to see Aunt Madge and Uncle Hector for a few days?' Her expression was deliberately bland.

He bit into a slice of buttered toast. 'After Quinn and Marni have gone, you mean,' he nodded.

'Well, actually,' she avoided his gaze, 'I thought I might go—tomorrow.' Colour heated her cheeks.

He straightened slowly. 'That wouldn't be very polite, darling,' he reproved.

She moistened her lips. 'Perhaps not, but it might be more—prudent,' she advised ruefully. 'And you know Aunt Madge and Uncle Hector are always inviting me. I'm sure they would love to have me for a visit.'

'I'm sure they would too, but——' His eyes narrowed. 'Did Quinn wait up for you last night? He said something about not being able to sleep, and so I told him to make free with the library . . .'

Her mouth twisted. 'From what I could tell he made pretty free with your whisky too!'

Her grandfather frowned. 'After the tension and exhaustion of the concert I'm sure he needed it,' he dismissed. 'He didn't "make free" with anything else, though, did he?'

Her eyes flashed. 'Really, Grandfather, your subtlety leaves a lot to be desired lately!'

'Well?'

She carefully put down her cup in its saucer. 'I do not spend the evening with one man and the night with another,' she bit out in a controlled voice.

'You haven't spoken to Giles yet?' He frowned his disapproval.

'No,' she snapped. 'And I don't intend to while your *guest* remains here! Really, Grandfather,' she stood up agitatedly. 'Can't you see that I just don't like the man, that it would have been better for all of us if you had just let him leave today as planned?'

'I like him, Lissy,' he sighed.

She felt guilty as he called her by the only shortened version of her name he had ever used, knowing how disturbed he must be to have used it at all. 'Then let me go to Aunt Madge and Uncle Hector,' she encouraged desperately.

'If it's what you want,' he accepted heavily. 'Although I don't know what we'll tell our guests.'

She gave a tight smile, utterly relieved that he had agreed to let her go. 'Just leave that to me,' she assured him.

'Elizabeth——'

'It will be all right.' She patted his hand, her smile bright now that she was to be allowed to escape from this impossible situation. 'We'll just tell the Taylors that my plans to leave for Portugal tomorrow were made weeks ago,' she dismissed. 'They can't possibly feel slighted by that.'

Her grandfather rubbed his hand consideringly across his chin. 'I suppose not,' he finally agreed. 'But I can't say I approve of your behaviour, darling.'

'I——'

'Good morning, everyone,' Marni breezed lightly into the room. 'Isn't it a glorious day?' she enthused as she helped herself to food from the platters. She grinned self-consciously as she sat down opposite Elizabeth's grandfather, her plate piled high with bacon and sausages and mushrooms. 'I don't know why, the air is much fresher and cleaner where we live in the mountains, but I can't seem to stop eating over here.'

'Maybe it's the way Cook prepares the food.' Elizabeth smiled indulgently, knowing she was going to miss this endearing little imp. It was a pity Marni happened to be Quinn's daughter; she would have liked to spend more time getting to know her. Her relationship to Quinn made that impossible.

'Maybe.' Marni tucked in with enjoyment. 'Was that a swimming pool I could see out of my bedroom window this morning?' she asked excitedly, once her initial hunger had been appeased. She was cool and pretty in the yellow sun-dress, her perfume light and elusive.

That perfume. Elizabeth would know it anywhere; it was her own favourite daytime perfume. And Marni was wearing it. Quinn had bought the perfume for his *daughter*!

She should have known, should have guessed it wouldn't suit any of the women he was reputed to date, all of them too sophisticated for the lightly elusive perfume. He had deliberately let her believe he had bought it for one of his women!

Or had she just *presumed* that, and he had chosen to let her go on believing it, deliberately teasing her!

'Elizabeth?'

She blinked dazedly as she realised Marni was still waiting for her to answer her question, colour heating her cheeks as she saw her grandfather's searching gaze on her.

'Yes, we have a pool,' she replied harshly in her agitation. 'It's rarely used, though,' she frowned.

'Oh.' Marni looked disappointed.

She smiled at the younger girl's expressive face. 'Which isn't to say it *can't* be used,' she added gently, rewarded by Marni's excited smile.

'Ooh, great.' Marni began to eat with enthusiasm once again.

'But you'll have to wait until that breakfast has gone down, young lady,' Elizabeth's grandfather sternly warned the younger girl.

'Wait for what?'

Elizabeth turned sharply at the mild query; she just couldn't help herself, looking at Quinn with guarded eyes.

The last time she had seen him he had taunted her

about wanting him, and as she witnesssed how ruggedly attractive he looked this morning she knew the accusation had been true. How could he still look so handsome to her when she knew the truth about him!

He oozed sexuality without even trying, dark and virile after the shower he seemed to have taken since his horse-ride, his hair brushed back damply, a light blue shirt and faded denims moulded to the hard muscles of his body. He might spend a lot of time in a recording studio working on the albums he put out half-yearly, might have cut down on the actual public appearances he did now, but he had certainly found some other way to keep fit.

But he looked tired today, evidence that he had spent what had been left of the night after they parted as restlessly as Elizabeth.

'The estate has a pool, Daddy,' Marni was the one to answer him exictedly. 'We're all going to have a swim once our breakfast has gone down.'

Elizabeth's eyes widened in protest as she registered the statement. 'Oh, but I——'

'Sounds like a good idea,' Quinn drawled as he strode lazily into the room. 'I think I'll join you two ladies,' he murmured, his gaze fixed challengingly on Elizabeth.

What was he doing? They had nothing left to say to each other after last night, had said it all then, and yet the mockery in his eyes dared her to go swimming with him and Marni.

Last night she had told this man she hated him, had explained exactly why she felt that way; he couldn't expect the two of them just to carry on today as if nothing had transpired between them to change their roles of polite hostess and guest!

But looking at him now, as he sat down beside his daughter to eat his breakfast, still looking up at *her* challengingly, she knew that was exactly what he intended doing!

CHAPTER EIGHT

'SHE swims well, doesn't she?' Quinn gazed proudly at his daughter as she swam several laps of the pool. 'She would like an outside pool at the house,' he shrugged. 'But it wouldn't be all that practical when we're surrounded by snow six months of the year.'

'Quinn, what are you doing?' she demanded harshly.

Against her better judgement she had been persuaded by Marni to join them at the pool, and had instantly found herself alone with Quinn as Marni dived smoothly into the clear warm water.

Quinn had calmly offered her a glass of the cooled lemonade that had been brought out for their enjoyment, and within seconds she found herself lying on the lounger beside his.

From his conversation he was determined to act as if nothing had changed between them, but she couldn't be that sophisticated!

He turned to her with raised brows. 'I thought I was talking about Marni,' he drawled.

'Why?' she choked.

He shrugged. 'If you don't agree with me about Marni's swimming, then just say so,' he said.

Just being here with him like this disturbed her. The blue bathing trunks he wore were almost indecent in their lack of material, and from the way his body seemed to be tanned all over he didn't always bother with those! She didn't want to be disturbed by his raw masculinity, but she couldn't seem to help herself.

'Why are you talking about Marni at all?' she said agitatedly. 'You have to realise that neither one of us is really interested in how well she swims!'

'I'm sorry you feel that way,' he murmured. 'I thought you liked Marni.'

'I do!' she snapped impatiently. 'But you and I have *nothing* left to say to each other!'

He calmly took a sip of his lemonade, the ice cubes clinking against the side of the frosted glass. 'We have plenty left to say to one another,' he told her softly, his gaze suddenly intent. 'And when you're prepared to listen, when you *want* to know, I'll tell you,' he said intently. 'But in the meantime,' he added briskly. 'Isn't the weather pleasant for this time of year?'

She gave a heavy sigh. 'It isn't going to work, Quinn.'

He raised his brows. 'What isn't?' he enquired mildly.

'This,' she sat forward. 'Why on earth did you accept my grandfather's invitation when you know how much I want you gone from here?'

He shrugged. 'Although you may not believe this right now,' he murmured, 'I don't plan my life around tormenting you!'

'I *don't* believe it,' she rasped.

Quinn sighed. 'Lise, I had no way of knowing who you were when I arranged to come here.' He ignored the way she flinched at the use of Fergus's name for her. 'God, I still didn't recogise you completely when I first met Elizabeth Farnham. All I knew was that you struck a chord in my memory. A pleasant chord,' he added softly.

'What a pity I can't remember the incident the same way,' she snapped scornfully.

His expression was gentle. 'You enjoyed the kiss we shared as much as I did,' he chided.

'I barely remember the kiss,' she lied. 'It's completely overshadowed by what came later.'

'By what you think came later,' he corrected.

'I *heard* what came later,' she reminded him harshly. 'I suppose it must hint at some sign of decency on your part that you arranged to leave the next day rather than continue your sordid little affair under my aunt and uncle's roof,' she scorned. 'It might have been a little difficult for Terri to claim I prevented her going to Fergus's every night of your stay with us by being such a pest as to stay awake!'

'You did have your ear pressed against the door that night, didn't you,' Quinn derided.

'In her haste to get into bed with you Terri didn't close the door properly behind her!' she defended.

'And I left the next day because my wife of the last ten years had filed the divorce papers while I was conveniently out of the country,' he revealed bleakly. 'She threatened to take my daughter away from me unless I gave her everything she asked for in the settlement.'

Elizabeth looked at him without sympathy. 'And what did she ask for in the settlement?'

He gave a harsh laugh. 'Everything but the clothes I stood up in!'

'"A woman scorned",' Elizabeth mocked.

His eyes flared with anger. 'I told you I was always faithful to my wife.'

'Then why did she leave you?' she asked.

'She didn't leave me,' he ground out. 'I left her. I——'

'Hi, you two,' Marni leant her arms on the edge of the pool as she gazed up at them, her hair slicked back darkly as water fell in rivulets down her face and body. 'Aren't you coming in?'

'Soon,' her father answered her. 'Li—Elizabeth and I are just talking.'

She gave them a speculative look. 'Oh, sure!' She gave a mischievous grin before turning back into the water, moving off with powerful strokes.

Quinn drew in a ragged breath as he watched her. 'She isn't mine.'

Elizabeth's eyes widened at the painfully made statement, meeting his gaze frowningly. He couldn't really have just said—it wasn't possible that—Marni obviously adored her father! He couldn't have meant what she had thought he had!

He turned to her with dark eyes. 'She isn't mine, Lise,' he repeated raspingly. 'I was with Maggie all through the pregnancy, watched Marni being born, changed her diapers as often as Maggie did,' he remembered ruefully. 'It was me she walked to when she took her first steps; "Daddy" was the first word she spoke. I loved her so much, was so proud when people commented that they could see this or that likeness between us.' He shook his head emotionally. 'How Maggie must have secretly laughed every time someone said something like

that,' he rasped. 'Marni isn't a damned bit like me—
because she isn't my daughter!'

Elizabeth just looked at him, not knowing what to
say, realising there was nothing *she* could say.

'Nearly seven years ago,' he spoke flatly now,
'Marni was involved in an accident, she needed a
blood-transfusion. I—I offered them my blood,' his
face was bleak as he relived the memory. 'Do you
know what they said?' he rasped, his eyes full of
pain. 'They said that my blood wasn't compatible
with Marni's, but that it wasn't surprising as I
wasn't her real father. Marni was growing weaker
by the moment and there wasn't a damned thing I,
the man who couldn't possibly have fathered her,
could do about it!' he groaned. 'They took the blood
from the supplies they already had, and Maggie
explained to me that the man who had been my bass
guitarist when I first started out had fathered
Marni. I remembered him then, a silver-haired kid
who believed the world could be his if he wanted it!
Well he certainly had my wife,' he stated bitterly.
'Although, apparently, he wasn't unique in that!'

Elizabeth swallowed hard. It was nothing like her
own situation; there had been no loving father, even
one that wasn't really her own, in her life. And yet
she suddenly felt a deep affinity with Marni. She
tried not to feel anything at all for Quinn, knowing
she couldn't even afford to give him pity.

'Does Marni know?' she prompted.

He shook his head. 'She's never going to, either,'
he bit out. 'In every way that matters I am her
father; I just no longer have a wife. Hell, I might
even have been able to forgive Maggie if she had

come and told me the truth when she first discovered she was pregnant. But I could never forgive all those years she let me go on believing a lie. And I guess she showed what was really important to her when she exchanged her daughter for money and property.'

Elizabeth moistened her lips. 'If even Marni doesn't know the truth, why—why did you tell me?'

He sighed. 'Maybe I'm trying to explain to you what frame of mind I was in when I came to London six years ago, trying to make you realise how I——'

'You expect me to excuse your behaviour with Terri because your marriage had broken down and you didn't give a damn who you hurt?' she said incredulously.

'I'm not talking about Terri at all!' he dismissed harshly. 'Forget about Terri. I want——'

'I can't forget about Terri,' she shook her head. 'I could never forget about you and her.'

'There never was any me and her.' His voice rose angrily. 'I'm talking about you and me here!'

'You and me?' she echoed disbelievingly. 'Come on, Quinn, a birthday kiss for an impressionable seventeen-year-old doesn't add up to any you and me!'

'It was the kiss that came after the birthday kiss that's important,' Quinn rasped. 'I was disgusted by my behaviour with a kid that didn't look much older than my own daughter——'

'And so you took up Terri's offer—once again,' she scorned, standing up. 'Thanks for telling me all this, Quinn—and your relationship to Marni will go no further than me—but none of this changes how I

feel about you,' she dismissed. 'You're a selfish,
egotistical swine who helped force Fergus to his
death.'

'No!'

'Yes.' She didn't back away from him as he stood
up to tower over her. 'Thankfully, after tomorrow, I
don't have to see you again,' she added with
satisfaction.

His brows rose. 'But I accepted your grandfather's invitation to stay on,' he reminded softly.

'And *I'm* going to stay with my aunt and uncle,'
she announced triumphantly, feeling immensely
satisfied as he frowned darkly.

'No!' he finally rasped.

'Oh, yes,' she nodded firmly. 'And I won't be
returning until after you have left. Would you like
me to say hello to my aunt and uncle for you?' she
added harshly. 'They still think you're Mr
Wonderful!'

'I expected to see them while I was here,' he
sighed wearily. 'My lawyer never mentioned that
they had moved.'

'Maybe he didn't think you were interested,' she
said.

Quinn's mouth tightened. 'Oh, I was interested, I
just didn't want to bring back any painful memories
by—— Your running away won't solve anything,'
he warned harshly.

'I'm not running, Quinn,' she bit out coldly.
'This time I *am* walking.'

She didn't expect him to try and stop her as she
left the pool area, and he didn't. They had finally
said all that needed to be said.

She did feel for him over the shock he must have received when he learnt of Marni's true paternity, knew her own situation had been slightly reversed, but the shock of finding out who her father *was* at that late stage in her life couldn't have been so different from Quinn learning he wasn't Marni's father after all.

But none of that excused his behaviour with Terri!

'It's a bit sudden, isn't it, darling?' Giles complained.

She had driven over after lunch to tell him about her planned visit to her aunt and uncle, deciding not to wait until tonight to see him after all. 'Not really,' she dismissed. 'I've been meaning to go for some time.'

'But even so——' He looked up as one of the girls who helped out in the stables knocked on the door.

'There's a visitor for you, Mr Soper,' she informed him a little breathlessly.

Giles looked irritated, although Sunday afternoon was usually one of his busiest times for visits from the owners of his horses.

'I'll make myself scarce,' Elizabeth offered lightly, picking up her burgundy-coloured bag that exactly matched the shading of the burgundy and cream dress she wore.

'That might not be necessary,' Giles dismissed impatiently, obviously having decided their conversation about her proposed visit to her aunt and uncle was far from over. He turned back to the girl. 'Who is it, Sheila?'

'I hope you don't mind, Soper.' Quinn appeared behind the girl, his gaze sweeping disturbingly over Elizabeth before concentrating on the other man. 'But you did say I could come over and have a look around some time.'

She should have guessed, should have recognised that dreamy look on Sheila's face; it was the same look Mary had on *her* face whenever she had chanced to see Quinn Taylor!

And she didn't for a moment believe he had come here just to look at horses!

Although he was certainly dressed for the part as he came further into the room. The riding-boots were obviously his own, but the jacket and jodpurs certainly looked very much like her grandfather's. Considering the two men were of a similar build she wouldn't be surprised. She also wouldn't put it past her grandfather to have told Quinn where she had gone; he wasn't going to give up until the last possible moment, the old devil, no matter what he had said to the contrary!

'Of course, of course.' Giles greeted the other man effusively, dismissing the stable-girl with a flick of his hand, giving her an irritated frown as she continued to stare at Quinn. The poor girl left with a self-conscious blush. Elizabeth didn't doubt that by the time the two men emerged out into the stables the whole workforce would be looking out for Quinn Taylor!

'It's quite a set-up you seem to have here,' Quinn murmured appreciatively.

Giles looked pleased by the compliment—as he was no doubt supposed to, Elizabeth thought bitchily. Quinn gave her a mocking look. She met his gaze unflinchingly.

'If I had known you were coming, Mr Taylor, we could have driven over together,' she drawled.

'I had no idea where you were going when you disappeared straight after lunch,' he returned tauntingly.

Her mouth tightened. She hadn't exactly disappeared after lunch so much as made an escape, anxious to be away from the house. She hadn't expected Quinn to follow her. He was really starting to be annoying, always appearing when she least expected him to, just—just always *there*! And he was doing it on purpose, really seemed to think there could be something between them. He finally saw her as a woman, and it was too late, six years too late.

'Please, gentlemen, don't let me keep you,' she encouraged them lightly. 'I'm sure the two of you are longing to look over Giles's Arabians.'

'Come with us,' Quinn urged softly. 'I promise I won't even let a horse near you,' he added teasingly.

She stiffened at the taunt. 'No, thank you.' Her voice was saccharin-sweet. 'I'm hardly dressed for—walking around the stables.' She looked down pointedly at her burgundy-coloured high-heeled sandals and silky dress. 'I'll just wait for you here, Giles,' she gave him a warm smile, hoping Quinn would take the hint she had given that she didn't expect him to return to the house with the other man. But even if he had picked up the implication, he would probably do the exact opposite just to be annoying!

The mocking look he gave her as he left with Giles

told her he was more than capable of doing that.

She stood up to stare out of the window, absently watching the two men as they strolled together over to the stable complex that comprised Giles's stud and training facility. Why was Quinn here? What could he hope to gain by making a nuisance of himself like this?

And he was starting to become very annoying, just his presence bothering her. But then he knew that; why else would he be doing this? She wouldn't put it past him to follow her to Portugal too, on the pretext of seeing her aunt and uncle again, of course!

It was ironic really: once she would have given everything to have *Quinn Taylor* pursue her in this way, now she just wanted him to realise there was no point to it, that no matter what they felt for each other, be it desire on his side and love on hers, Fergus's death, the reason behind it, would always stand between them. She had to talk to him again before she left tomorrow, had to make him understand.

Why couldn't he *see* it was no use? Why did he keep tormenting them both this way?

CHAPTER NINE

ELIZABETH'S afternoon with Giles hadn't been a success. As she had known he would, Quinn came back to the house with the other man, the two of them enjoying a drink while they discussed the merits of Giles's horses. By the time she stood up to leave at four-thirty she was angry with both of them, with Quinn for monopolising most of their afternoon, and with Giles for letting him!

She had parted rather tersely from Giles outside, aware that Quinn could be—and probably was—watching them from the drawing-room window.

She had only managed to spend those few brief minutes alone with Giles before Quinn's arrival, hardly long enough to have explained to him that she didn't think it was a good idea to see each other once she returned from her visit to her aunt and uncle. And she had put off seeing him tonight.

'Someone upset you, darling?' her grandfather enquired innocently as she slammed the door behind her.

She glared across the entrance-hall at him. 'You know damn well they have,' she snapped. 'When are you going to stop your wily old fox act and realise Quinn and I just aren't suited!'

He arched wary brows. 'He mentioned that Giles had invited him over some time, and so I——'

'Encouraged him to go over today!' she finished tightly.

'No, darling,' he rebuked gently. 'I just gave him the directions to Giles's house when he asked for them.'

Her anger towards him fled as quickly as it had come, and she launched herself into his arms with a tormented sob. 'He keeps following me, Grandfather,' she choked. 'I can't seem to make him understand that I can't care for him.'

'Can't?' he echoed softly. 'Darling——'

'Don't want to,' she amended firmly as she pulled out of his arms. 'I'm not the type for a brief affair,' she pointed out lightly, realising she must get a grip on herself. 'And I'm certainly not interested in marriage with a man like Quinn Taylor,' she dismissed mockingly.

Her grandfather smiled. 'You must be the only woman who isn't!'

Was that why Quinn was so determined to have her, because unlike most women she hadn't fallen into his arms? Thinking back to just how many times she *had* been in his arms the last few days she couldn't believe that was true!

'Now you wouldn't want me to go and live in Canada, would you?' she teased her grandfather.

He frowned. 'I wouldn't like it, no ... But if Quinn is the man you want I wouldn't stand in your way.' He shook his head.

'He isn't,' she lightly dismissed. 'So don't even think about it. Now how about some afternoon tea?' She put her arm companionably through his, the subject of Quinn dropped.

'What happened to you two this afternoon?' Marni enquired curiously as they all sat around the dinner table.

Quinn gave Elizabeth an amused glance as she almost choked on her beef at being grouped together with him as if they were a couple. 'We drove over to take a look at Mr Soper's stud-farm,' he drawled.

Elizabeth gave him a censorious frown. 'What your father means is that he drove over and met Giles and me there,' she corrected tightly.

Marni gave a dismissive shrug, as if their method of getting there didn't really interest her. 'I wish I'd known, I would have loved to have gone too.'

'Maybe next time, honey,' her father consoled her. 'Mr Soper has given us an invitation to go over any time we like,' he explained at Marni's excited expression.

He made it sound as if he intended their stay to be a prolonged one. And much as she was looking forward to staying with her aunt and uncle, and knew they were looking forward to having her, she couldn't stay on with them indefinitely.

'How much longer do you think you'll be in England, Mr—Quinn?' she amended stiffly at his narrow-eyed look.

The amusement suddenly left his expression, and he gave a shrug. 'It depends,' he finally answered.

She didn't need to ask 'on what'; she could see clearly from the look in his eyes that the way things were between them had a lot to do with when, and if, he left England.

'Well, if you leave before my return from Portugal I hope you have a pleasant journey,' she returned politely.

'It sure is a pity that you have to go away tomorrow,' Marni voiced her disappointment with the arrangement. 'I thought you and I would be able to spend some more time together, maybe go out shopping again.'

Elizabeth glanced sharply at Quinn, wondering if he had put his daughter up to this, knowing by his frowning look that he hadn't, instantly feeling guilty for misjudging Marni.

She touched the young girl's hand lightly. 'Maybe next time your father is in England,' she encouraged huskily. Marni's liking for her was completely reciprocated.

The young girl grimaced. 'I'll probably be back in school by then.'

Elizabeth shifted her gaze uncomfortably from her grandfather's censorious one as she guessed that the reason for it was the impetuosity of her decision to visit her aunt and uncle. He didn't know, couldn't understand—— She didn't like hurting Marni either, but to avoid the father she unfortunately had to avoid the daughter too.

'Perhaps you won't be,' she dismissed lightly.

'Maybe not.' Marni sounded unconvinced.

'Shall we go through for coffee?' she prompted brightly, a sudden heaviness having fallen over them all.

'Not for us.' Quinn was suddenly standing at the back of her chair pulling it back for her, his hand firm on her arm as she automatically stood, holding her against his side. 'Marni can pour for you,' he told her grandfather. 'It will be good practice for her.' He grinned at his daughter. 'She tells me she likes this sort of life and intends finding herself a lord or some other titled man so that she can continue to live the gracious life to which she is fast becoming accustomed!'

'Dad!' Marni protested with red-faced embarrassment. 'Anyway,' she added cheekily, 'he doesn't have to be titled; just have a house like this and pots of money to spend on it and me!'

'I think I rather fit that bill,' Elizabeth's grandfather drawled. 'I am sorry about the lack of an actual title, though. But perhaps we can come to some sort of arrangement?' he added teasingly, placing Marni's hand firmly in the crook of his arm as they walked off in the direction of the drawing room, still talking about that 'arrangement'.

Elizabeth stared after them dazedly. The conversation had too many serious undertones for her liking. Oh, not that she believed her grandfather was seriously offering for Marni, that would be ludicrous considering he was old enough to be her *great*-grandfather, but she wouldn't put it past her grandfather to issue the younger girl a standing invitation to come and stay here whenever she wanted to!

'Let them go,' Quinn instructed softly as she would have called out to the other couple. 'Marni's having the time of her life,' he smiled indulgently. 'And your grandfather is enjoying himself.'

She could see that, he and Marni laughing softly together as he closed the drawing-room door.

'Unless, of course, you're jealous?'

She turned sharply to Quinn, anger darkening her eyes to the colour of shaded emeralds. 'What do you——'

'I guess you're pretty used to having your grandfather all to yourself, eh?' he looked at her consideringly.

'Don't be ridiculous.' The anger flushed her cheeks. 'I just—I was concerned that—my grandfather likes you both, and——'

'You don't want us back here,' he finished softly. 'Don't worry, Lise, if I leave here without you this time I'm going to wait for you to come to me.'

She gave a scornful laugh. 'You'll have a long time to wait then because I don't intend—or want—to see you again!'

He nodded, unperturbed by her vehemence. 'I can understand that.'

'How clever of you!'

'*You* don't understand,' he said ruefully. 'Or maybe you just don't want to yet.' He sighed. 'My wife cheated on me all the years of our marriage; the next woman that shares my life comes to me on my terms,' he added grimly.

'And what are your terms?' she couldn't resist asking, curious in spite of herself, having no intention of being the 'next woman to share his life'!

His mouth twisted. 'There's only one really, and it's going to be especially difficult for you.'

'Yes?' she prompted breathlessly.

Quinn shook his head. 'Half the difficulty for you is going to be in realising what it is,' he sighed.

'I—what are you doing?' she cried protestingly as he swung her up in his arms and began walking up the stairs.

He glanced down at her, his eyes bleak. 'I can't depend on your realising what it is I want of you, and so I'm claiming one night with you. A night that may have to last me the rest of my life,' he added harshly.

He had been speaking in riddles for most of the last five minutes, and she couldn't pretend to understand what it was he thought he wanted of her, but she understood his intent now only too well, struggling in his arms to be put down.

'Don't, Lise.' The raw hunger of his tone stilled her, and she stared up at him dazedly. 'One night, that's all I'm asking,' he repeated raspingly.

Her gaze was locked with his, her struggles ceased. Not this man, she couldn't make love with this man. Out of all the men she could have chosen to fall in love with why did it have to be him! She couldn't give him this night, daren't give him this night. And yet how could she say no to one night with him, a night that *would* have to last her all her life, when she loved him so much?

'You know,' he knelt beside her as he laid her down on her bed in the darkened bedroom, 'you could do with losing a few pounds.' He gave an exaggerated sigh of relief at being able to release his burden.

Temper darkened her eyes. 'You——'

'That's it,' he grinned as he pinioned her hands by the sides of her head as he laid the full length of his body on hers, making her fully aware of the hardness of his chest and thighs. 'Fight, Lise. Bite and scratch, give me all the passion you have!'

She shook her head agitatedly from side to side. 'I don't want——'

'Yes, you do, Lise,' he encouraged harshly. 'You want me so much you're burning with it!'

She did, and she was! Her whole body was aflame with wanting him, and she pressed her hips against him as she felt the throb of his arousal.

One night . . . Could she forgive herself for taking this one night? She would have to live with that question later, right now her body was reacting instinctively to the caress of Quinn's mouth!'

The warmth of his breath was a caress against her skin as his lips probed the hollows of her throat, nibbling on the lobe of the ear, only slowly releasing her hands as he felt her surrender to his mastery.

Her hands slid caressingly about his neck, clasping his shoulders as his mouth claimed her, fused together as their tongues fought a duel where they both emerged the victor.

She caressed his back, loving the hard muscled strength of him, gasping as he deftly unfastened her scarlet gown to caress the hardened nub of her breast with the moist heat of his tongue.

Her back arched in sudden need, her head thrown back as the sensual pleasure washed over her.

'So silken. So soft,' Quinn groaned as his hands moved gently over her nakedness, touching the slender dip of her waist, the curve of her hip. 'So soft here.' His hand gently cupped the throbbing mound beneath curling golden hair.

She breathed raggedly, meeting his open-mouthed kiss, moving against him in a sensual agony.

It was happening too fast, was completely out of control. She needed him, oh God, how she needed him!

She gasped as his mouth once again latched on to her nipple, caressing the puckered peak with his lips, his tongue, his teeth. The last sent an erotic charge through her body, trembling as the double assault on her senses made her tremble convulsively against him.

She sobbed out a broken moan as the ache between her thighs threatened to burn her, to send them both up in flames.

'Easy,' Quinn quietened her, soothing the wild tumult of her body with his gently soothing caresses. 'You'll be all right, Lise, I won't hurt you. I only want to love you,' he groaned, stripping his shirt from his body, his chest darkly virile in the shadowed room, slowly easing himself back on top of her, the dark hair on his chest a sensual caress in itself.

'Now, Quinn,' she urged raggedly. 'Please love me now. I—I hurt so much,' she admitted brokenly.

His eyes darkened, his lips gentle against first one breast and then the other. 'Soon,' he murmured against her lips. 'Soon, my love.'

Every time he touched her now it seemed she

convulsed with an aching fire, turning her passion
on him as she began to caress him in the way he had
her, discovering that a man's nipples could be as
sensitive as a woman's, Quinn offering no resistance
as she pushed him back on the bed, following him
down, her hair falling silkily on to his chest as she
kissed and suckled against him the way his lips had
taught her.

His hand tightly gripped the back of her head as
his breathing came in hoarse gasps, her lips
following the pattern of the hair on his chest, giving
him gentle kisses and nips with her teeth as she
followed the dark vee of hair to his navel. She paused
there, wondering if he would allow her to go lower,
longing to caress him as intimately there too as he
had her.

'Eve!' he groaned as he pulled her on top of him,
his hand cupping her nape as he brought her lips
down on to his.'

She winced slightly as the hardness of him pressed
into her through his trousers, pulsing restlessly.
God, he was so big, so hard, she——

'What is it?' Quinn frowned up at her as he sensed
her sudden panic, searching the pallor of her cheeks.
'Lise?' he questioned uncertainly.

She swallowed hard, could still feel him moving
against her, the thin material of his trousers the only
barrier against him thrusting between her thighs.

'Lise?' he prompted again, gently lowering her to
the bed beside him, leaning across her to switch on
the bedside lamp, his hands cradling either side of
her face as he searched her darkened green eyes. 'My

God,' he breathed slowly, his voice gruff with awe. 'I wanted a night with you,' he drew in a controlling breath. 'But I won't take *that* from you.' He shook his head.

'Quinn——'

He gave a self-derisive groan, rolling on to his back, his arm across his forehead. 'It's all right, Lise,' he comforted gruffly. 'The—the pain—the need, will go. If—*when* you come to Canada I want you to bring your virginity with you.' He sat up, moving away from her to sit on the side of the bed, deliberately not looking at her. 'It's the ultimate gift, isn't it,' he breathed raggedly as he stood up to pull on his white dress-shirt.

Elizabeth watched him with pained eyes, slowly pulling the quilt over her nakedness. She turned to lean on her elbow, swallowing convulsively. 'I—I seriously doubt I'll ever come to you in Canada, Quinn,' she told him truthfully.

'All the more reason for me not to take your innocence.' He thrust his shirt tail into his trousers, his hands shaking slightly as he did up the buttons.

She shook her head. 'I don't understand you, Quinn.'

And she didn't. She had been his for the taking, willing, *eager*, would have forgotten that momentary nervousness once he began caressing her again.

But he had been the one to draw a halt to their lovemaking, had had her at his mercy but chosen not to take her. Because he learnt of her innocence.

He looked at her with darkly disturbed eyes, picking up his jacket to leave. 'Maybe this will help you.' He paused at the door. 'Six years ago I was attracted to a young girl who couldn't accept me for what I was when I fell off the pedestal she had placed me on. When I arrived here less than a week ago I was instantly attracted to Elizabeth Farnham, didn't realise at first that Lise and Elizabeth were the same woman. By the time I had realised it, it was too late to change the way I feel about *both* of them; I can't take your virginity, Lise, because I'm in love with you.' He quietly left the room.

She stared at the closed door, her disbelief showing in her eyes.

Telling her he loved her hadn't 'helped' at all!

CHAPTER TEN

ELIZABETH stared at the birthday card as if it were about to bite her.

She had opened all her cards in complete innocence of the shock that was to come, hadn't really been all that interested in them, although she appreciated people's thoughtfulness in remembering her. But finally turning twenty-three hadn't seemed very important to her, just another miserable day, the last in a long line of many since she and Quinn had parted almost three weeks ago.

As usual, seeing her aunt and uncle had been pleasant, the three of them enjoying her visit. After a week she had come home, only to find that Quinn had left two days earlier. She had been pleased he was gone, she told herself, but as the days passed and she longed to see him again, she knew she was lying to herself.

And now he had remembered her birthday. The front of the card depicted the mountains he loved, and the message inside was brief and to the point, 'We're waiting. Quinn'.

Waiting for what? She still hadn't worked out what it was he wanted from her, what that single 'term' was that he expected of her. She did know she wanted to see him again, that the ache he had left her with hadn't lessened, that the pain hadn't gone away, as he had said it would. But there was no future for them if she did go to him, there never could be.

She put the card away in her bag before her grandfather saw it, knowing he would question the message inside it if he were to read it.

He had been concerned about her since she came back from her visit to Portugal, she knew that, had worried when she had stopped seeing Giles and began to spend all her evenings at home. She didn't want to worry him, hated to see that puzzlement in his eyes as he looked at her when he didn't think she was aware of it. But what could she tell him to reassure him, certainly not that she was in love with a man she could never be happy with!

And so she didn't tell him anything, and was more tense than ever this last week since she knew the concert filmed at the Hall was to be screened on Saturday. She didn't want to watch it, but she knew she wouldn't be able to stop herself, drawn as if by a magnet to watch Quinn, even if it were only on a television screen.

Her grandfather joined her just as the concert was about to start, giving her a smile as he made himself comfortable in the chair opposite hers.

Quinn looked so relaxed as he came out on the stage to thunderous applause, making it impossible to believe he had been so tense only minutes before at the house.

He had the audience in the palm of his hand from the first song, telling them of the love he had known yesterday, a spring love that hadn't lasted until summer.

Elizabeth gripped the side of her chair as he softly told the audience at the end of the song that it had been for 'a very special woman in his life, called Lise'.

Her mind was racing as she sensed her grandfather's questioning gaze on her, remembering the words of the song, suddenly realising that *she* had been spring when he first met her, that she was summer now. And Quinn believed she no longer loved him. Or, at least, not enough.

That was it! Quinn had told her there was only one condition to her going to him, and now she realised what it was; she had to love him enough to *trust* him, with that love, and over what had happened to Fergus. He had told her he hadn't had an affair with Terri, at her aunt's house or any other time, and despite what she had overheard, she had to love him enough to trust he told her the truth.

Did she love him enough for that?

'Elizabeth—or should I call you Lise?' her grandfather gently interrupted her tortuous thoughts. 'Why don't you go to him?'

She looked up at him with pained eyes. 'It isn't that simple,' she choked, shaking her head.

'Do you love him?'

'It isn't *that* simple either!' she dismissed derisively. 'If it were I would be with him now.'

Her grandfather looked at her frowningly, sitting forward to turn down the volume on the television set. 'Do you want to tell me about it?' he asked her gently. 'I told you, I'm ready to listen at any time.'

She gave a ragged sigh. 'Maybe I should tell you,' she nodded. 'My thoughts and feelings are so muddled I don't know what to do any more!'

'Start with how Quinn happens to call you Lise,' her grandfather prompted softly after the lengthy silence.

She gave a wan smile at his perception, finally finding the strength to begin talking, telling him about her first meeting with Quinn six years ago, about Fergus and Terri, about *Quinn* and Terri, and all that had come after that.

Her grandfather listened without comment until she got to the end, not even interrupting when she explained how she had realised she still loved Quinn. Although he did frown a little when she told him that Quinn had admitted to loving her too.

'He wants me to trust him, Grandfather,' she concluded in a shaky voice. 'And I'm just not sure that I can.'

Her grandfather released a ragged breath. 'I understand your reaction to my decision to allow the concert to be held here now,' he said ruefully. 'But aren't you assuming rather a lot about what took place in Canada five and a half years ago?' he encouraged gently.

She sighed. 'I didn't imagine hearing Quinn and Terri together in his room that night.'

'But Quinn has already told you that she didn't spend the night with him,' he reminded. 'Lise—I might as well call you that if everyone else is going to——'

She shook her head. 'Only Quinn. And I'm still not sure I'll ever see him again,' she added bleakly.

Her grandfather sighed. 'What you felt and saw six years ago was the love and reaction of a young girl,' he explained softly. 'You fell in love with an idol—You did, Lise,' he insisted gently. 'You didn't see the man so much as the star. And when that star fell to the ground and became no more than another vulnerable human you were more than willing, in your disenchantment, to believe the earth he had fallen to had tarnished him. Maybe you did hear Terri in his bedroom that night——'

'Oh, I did,' she remembered harshly.

'But you went back to your own room, have no idea what happened next. How do you know he didn't throw the young baggage out and she spent the rest of the night with your cousin?'

'Quinn said she must have done that ...' she recalled uncertainly.

'Then I believe him,' he grandfather said without hesitation.

It was amazing, her grandfather had spent barely a week in Quinn's company, and yet he trusted the other man's word implicitly. Why couldn't *she* be that sure?

'Darling, don't look so stricken,' her grandfather encouraged raggedly. 'All of this happnened when you were very young and impressionable, when black was black and white was white. I happen to think you would have been able to deal with it better when you were older, when you had time to consider what sort of man Quinn is. But in between your cousin's death and your full maturity you received another blow that made you doubt the sincerity of all men.' His expression was grim.

'Learning who my father was,' she realised slowly.

'And how he had ignored your existence since birth,' her grandfather added harshly. 'Your feelings for Quinn were never allowed to mature, to be seen through the more knowledgeable eyes of a woman. If they had you would have realised that he isn't the type of man to betray a friend, that he's a man who has been hurt himself in the past.'

And he certainly wouldn't have wanted to cause another man the same sort of pain of betrayal he had known from his wife!

He had tried to explain to her, to make her realise that, and she had once again chosen to misjudge him! Oh God, she had known all the facts, Quinn had told her the truth as much as his pride would allow, and she had refused to see it for what it was!

'What do I do now?' she cried as she ran across the room to her grandfather's waiting arms.

She didn't doubt any more, could see past the pain of her own father's betrayal, and knew that Quinn's only fault concerning Fergus's death, his only regret, had been that he hadn't been able to prevent it happening.

Her grandfather patted her back soothingly as she sobbed. 'I would say you call up the airport and get yourself booked on the first available flight to Canada.'

'What if he no longer wants me?' she choked.

'Quinn is the type of man who will "wait" for ever if he has to,' her grandfather assured her ruefully. 'And I insist on being there for the wedding,' he added sternly. 'I've missed most of the other important events in your life, I don't intend to miss that one.'

She gave a watery smile. 'Quinn has never mentioned marriage,' she reminded huskily. 'I think his first marriage soured him for the relationship.' She hadn't held anything back from her grandfather a few minutes ago, knowing that none of it would go any further.

'The man isn't a fool,' her grandfather derided. 'He isn't going to let a woman like you escape him!'

'I think you may be biased.' She gratefully took the handkerchief he handed her, blowing her nose and drying her eyes.

'He'll marry you,' her grandfather said with certainty. 'And I expect the first child to be named after his grandfather,' he added arrogantly. 'And for him to come and take over here.'

Children. How she longed to give Quinn children, a son that looked just like him, another daughter he could spoil. She knew, no matter what the truth was about Marni's paternity, that she would always be Quinn's first-born. But he would love the children they had together too.

God, she had been a fool ever to believe that a man who would give up everything he possessed to claim custody of the daughter that wasn't even his, a child that a lot of men would have rejected once they knew the truth, could have destroyed Fergus by his selfishness. There had to be another explanation, and she was finally ready to hear it. She couldn't help but feel nervous about whether or not Quinn was still prepared to give it to her, despite what he had written in his card.

She had never been to Canada before, but as soon as she stepped off the plane at Calgary airport she felt an affinity for the country, probably because it was where the man she loved called home!

It had been a long flight, a tense one for Elizabeth as she wondered what awaited her at the end of her journey, acceptance or rejection.

Her grandfather had seen her off at the airport in London, full of reassurances that everything would work out fine. But those reassurances had faded as soon as she got on to the plane that was to take her to Quinn, and as each mile passed her doubts increased. Quinn had been hurt so much in the past by what his wife had done to him, *she* had openly scorned him and any explanation about his behaviour he had tried to make; he would be perfectly within his rights to reject her.

Maybe that was why she had chosen not to tell him of her visit, hoping he would have more difficulty saying no to her if they were face to face.

As she drove her hire-car along the highway that took her up into the mountains her trepidation grew. What if she couldn't even get past the security that no doubt surrounded Quinn's home? Maybe she should have called from the airport to let him know she was on her way. She was going to look very silly if the guards wouldn't even admit her!

It was too late now, she decided with new determination. If Quinn wouldn't admit her she would just sit outside until he did.

It wasn't difficult to find the Taylor ranch as it nestled amongst the towering mountains, and as Elizabeth drove down the driveway that led to the main gate she could see she had been right about the security; two men blocked her path as she approached the wooden ranch-gate.

They were dressed in uniforms that clearly proclaimed them security-guards, the elder of the two coming to stand beside the car as she wound down her window.

'Do you have an appointment, ma'am?' he enquired politely, although the muscles bulging in his arms and chest were a little intimidating.

'Er—no——'

'Mr Taylor doesn't see anyone without an appointment.' He began to shake his head regretfully, as if he were well accustomed to having to turn away over-eager fans who tried to crash the little privacy Quinn managed to grab for himself.

He didn't look as if he could be persuaded to make an exception in her case either! 'Perhaps if you called the house,' she looked pointedly at the radio clipped to the top pocket of his shirt. 'And asked Mr Taylor if he would see——'

'It wouldn't do any good, ma'am——'

'—Elizabeth Farnham,' she finished awkwardly, realising her pleas weren't going to get her anywhere with this man and his partner.

But at the mention of her name the man's attitude suddenly had a transformation!

'I'm sorry, Miss Farnham,' he apologised profusely, turning hurriedly to his partner. 'Open the gate, Harry,' he instructed tersely before his gaze returned to Elizabeth. 'I had no idea who you were,' he explained hastily. 'Hurry it up, Harry,' he ordered harshly while still smiling at Elizabeth.

She frowned at this sudden change of attitude. 'Mr Taylor is—expecting me?' she said uncertainly. Had her grandfather called Quinn after all and told him of her plans in spite of her request that he didn't do so?

'Not exactly,' the man standing beside her smiled, his partner having opened the gate now. 'We just have instructions to admit you at any time.'

He didn't add 'night or day', but she could clearly see the speculation in his eyes as she gave him a non-committal smile before accelerating the car through the gate and up the driveway to the main house.

Pine trees edged the road, their scent heady and clean. And because of their density along the driveway she didn't see the ranch until she was almost upon it, her eyes widening appreciatively.

It was a one-storey wooden structure, built from the same trees that surrounded it on every side, the sturdy trunks stripped and enmeshed to form a log-cabin effect. Except that this house was much larger than any cabin had ever been. It was an incredibly beautiful house, the trees only thinned slightly to one side of it to allow for the grazing of the half-dozen horses that watched her approach curiously. Even her untrained eye could recognise the two Arabians Quinn had spoken of owning, sleek, beautiful creatures with an arrogant stance that spoke of their breeding.

She breathlessly recognised that she was wasting time, putting off the moment when she had to face Quinn; she had flown all these thousands of miles to see him, unsure of whether or not he would want to see her after all, and now she was trembling so badly she wasn't sure she was going to be able to get out of the car and walk up the steps to the front door.

'Elizabeth!'

She turned sharply at the excited greeting, relaxing slightly as Marni came exuberantly towards her. Obviously the guards had radioed the house and told them of her arrival. So, where was Quinn?

Marni hugged her as she got out on to the driveway, and she returned the greeting warmly.

'Am I glad to see you,' the younger girl said ruefully. 'Dad's been impossible to live with since we left England—and you,' she added pointedly.

She swallowed hard. 'Er—where is your father?'

'In the studio,' Marni grimaced, taking hold of her arm to drag her towards the house. 'Boy, is he going to be pleased to know you're here!'

Elizabeth came to halt just inside the door. 'He doesn't know I'm here yet?' she said nervously.

Marni shook her head impishly. She was wearing shorts and a T-shirt, and was very tanned from the hours she obviously spent outside. 'I thought about rushing in and telling him when Mike radioed that you were just passing through the main gate, but then I figured it would probably be more of a surprise if you were to just walk in on him yourself,' she announced triumphantly.

Surprise might not be the right description of Quinn's reaction to seeing her again, and Elizabeth couldn't help wishing that Marni had followed through on her first thought! Oh well, she had come this far, another few yards wasn't going to make that much difference.

'Where is this studio?' she prompted in a strained voice.

'At the back of the house, Dad had it built a couple of years ago,' Marni supplied conversationally as she led the way through the charmingly comfortable house, paintings of Indians hanging on the walls, the furniture itself of a style that could only be called rustic. But anything else would have looked ridiculous in this beautiful setting, rugged mountains visible as far as the eye could see. 'Like it?' Marni asked as she saw her admiring glances as they passed through each room.

'It's lovely,' she answered unhesitatingly.

'Hmm,' Marni agreed without conceit, 'Of course it isn't the original house we had here,' she added with a grimace. 'Mommy claimed that in the divorce and then sold it to some reclusive author. But this house is nicer than that one anyway,' she brightened, dismissing the subject of her mother from her mind, her eyes sparkling deeply blue. 'Dad designed this himself, and the studio.'

They had finally reached the end of the house, a long corridor leading to another section that would have been completely separate from the main house if it weren't for that.

'It can get pretty cold in the winter.' Marni explained the corridor, sobering suddenly. 'About Dad,' she began hesitantly. 'He's going to be thrilled to see you and everything, but—well, he's been so—unlike himself, since we got back,' she grimaced expressively. 'His music is sad, like it was when he and Mommy first parted,' she frowned.

Because she had hurt him too, perhaps even more than Maggie Taylor had.

'But you're here to change all that—aren't you?' Marni asked hopefully.

She smiled at the younger girl. 'I'm going to try,' she said shakily. 'With your permission, I hope?'

'Are you kidding?' the young girl grinned. 'It would be great to have a neat Mom like you!'

Elizabeth hugged the younger girl gratefully. 'Wish me luck.' She straightened, her shoulders tense as she faced the door of the studio.

'Believe me, I do,' Marni said fervently. 'But I don't think you'll need it,' she added softly just as Elizabeth's hand touched the studio door.

She turned to give her a rueful smile, swallowing nervously as she turned the handle of the door, going quietly into the room. Not that she thought Quinn would have heard or seen her entrance; it had become obvious as she opened the door that he was in the middle of singing one of those sad songs Marni had talked about, his back towards the door as he accompanied himself on the piano.

His voice was as rich and clear as it had always been; it was the words he was singing that were so disturbing. It wasn't like one of his usual songs, consisting of a jumbled series of lines that made her wonder if he were quite sober.

Suddenly his fingers came crashing down on the keys, leaning forward to rest his head on top of the piano.

Elizabeth forgot about the song and the disturbing message it seemed to give, running to his side as she sensed his despair. 'Quinn, I——'

He whirled round on the piano stool just as her hand reached out to him tentatively, and she was able to see how the last weeks had affected him, his eyes dark with unhappiness, his cheeks slightly hollow where he didn't seem to have bothered too much with food, lines of bitterness beside his mouth.

He stood up slowly, staring at her as if he weren't quite sure she were real—but didn't want to wake up if she weren't!

'It's really me, Quinn,' she told him gruffly. 'I—I grew up.'

He breathed raggedly. 'And?'

She swallowed hard. 'And I learnt how to trust,' she said shakily.

Still he held himself back. 'You're sure?'

'Sure enough to know that whatever happened six years ago, and then here later on, you didn't betray Fergus's friendship for you. I love you, Quinn,' she added without hesitation. 'I'm a little late admitting that—but not too late, I hope.' She looked up at him with widely uncertain eyes.

His answer was to open his arms to her, gathering her close against him as she went into them eagerly, his heart beating an erratic tattoo as Elizabeth rested her head against his chest.

'I thought you would never come,' he admitted raggedly into her hair. 'Each day has seemed like a year,' he added harshly. 'And I wasn't sure how much longer I could stay away from you!'

She looked up at him frowningly, at his dear, beloved face, smoothing away the frown from between his eyes. 'You would have come to me if I hadn't come to you?' She shook her head in slow disbelief.

He gave a rueful smile, cupping either side of her face with his beautiful hands. 'I wouldn't have been able to stay away. I've hungered for this.' He kissed her fiercely. 'And this,' the second kiss had gentled a little. 'And this!' he groaned as their lips met in drugging hunger.

Every ounce of love she possessed for this man went into that kiss, the loneliness of every second they had been apart, both of them breathing raggedly as they finally pulled slightly apart to gaze into each other's eyes, their feelings for each other so easily read there.

'I was wrong,' he said shakily. 'The hunger and need didn't go away,' he admitted shakily.

'For me neither.' She trembled in his arms.

'I wanted you all those years ago too, you know,' he told her gruffly. 'But you were young, too young, and so I left without ever telling you that you had helped heal me after the pain of my marriage break-up. You were so open and honest about your feelings,' he explained at her questioning look. 'You made me feel whole again. But you were too young for me, and in a way I was relieved when I got the telephone call that brought me back here. Six months later you looked at me with such hate that I knew that emotion was real too,' he sighed heavily.

'Because I held you responsible for Fergus's death,' she groaned. 'Believed you had had an affair with Terri.'

'I didn't,' he shook his head. 'Not ever. Although it was what she wanted. She did come to my room that night, had made it obvious in London before we came to your aunt's and uncle's house that she wanted me in her bed. I wasn't interested. Oh, she was beautiful enough, but she was also Fergus's girl, and he happened to love her, couldn't seem to see her for what she really was. And I hadn't touched a woman since my marriage had broken down,' he added softly. 'Or since. Except you.'

Elizabeth's eyes widened. 'But you were free,' she shook her head. 'What about all those women you've escorted in recent years?' she frowned.

'Sometimes it's necessary for me to attend social functions, for one reason or another. A female companion on those occasions seems to be essential. But I never made love to any of them.'

'Why not?' She still looked dazed, never doubting him.

'Because I didn't love them,' he shrugged. 'I have

to be in love with the woman I make love to.'

'But if you haven't made love for—in all that time,' she blushed. 'How were you able to—how did you——'

'Stop with you?' he finished teasingly. 'Believe me I suffered through hell for the rest of the night, and I wasn't feeling too comfortable the next day either. But, hell, I'd been celibate for seven years, what did another few weeks matter?' he asked.

'You were sure I would come to you?'

'No,' he admitted with a sigh. 'But as I told you, another few days and I wouldn't have been able to stay away.'

'I'm glad it happened this way,' she said softly. 'I don't want there to be any more doubts between us, and if you had come to me you would never have been sure.'

He shook his head. 'Maggie shook my faith in human nature, not in the woman I love.' He kissed her lingeringly. 'I think I loved you a little as Lise Morrison, and I love Elizabeth Farnham with my whole heart. The two together are a combination that would always have been able to defeat me!'

It was a long time before they could talk coherently again, Elizabeth curled up on Quinn's lap as he sat in the armchair in front of the window. But they still had so much to say, and their loving had already waited this long.

'The song you were singing when I came in,' she murmured against his chest, her fingers entangled in the dark hair she had revealed by unbuttoning his shirt. 'It sounded—disturbed.' She frowned up at him. 'Not at all like your usual music.'

He drew in a ragged breath. 'Because it wasn't mine,' he told her softly, smoothing her silky hair with loving fingers.

Her frown deepened. 'But I'm sure I've never heard it before . . .'

He shook his head. 'Because it was never released. And it never will be,' he added harshly. 'It was the song Fergus wrote before he—before he died.'

She straightened, looking at him questioningly. The song had been strange, talking about flowers and demons, the moon and—and *flying*. Off the top of a mountain!

'I should have seen what was coming,' Quinn berated himself fiercely. 'But at first I didn't even realise what was happening, and by the time I did it was too late to stop him. Fergus didn't want to stop,' he said heavily, lost in the memories.

'Fergus was high on drugs the night he died,' she realised brokenly.

'They both were, he and Terri.' He shook his head, defeated. 'At first I put his strange moods down to artistic temperament—God knows I have some moods myself! But with Fergus it went much deeper than that, and when I finally realised what was happening I tried to make him see what he was doing to himself, that if he got rid of the drugs he could continue to give pleasure to the world through his songs. For a while I think he did try to stop, but——'

'Yes?' Elizabeth prompted desperately.

He sighed. 'He had made too many contacts, too

many people who wanted to keep him addicted. And Terri didn't want to stop,' he added grimly.

'Couldn't she see what it was doing to Fergus?' Elizabeth said angrily.

'Not until it was too late.' He shook his head. 'And by that time Fergus was dead, and she was so hooked on the damned stuff that it took months of therapy to straighten her out. Her career never did pick up again, though.'

'She's a receptionist in a hotel in London,' Elizabeth supplied dully. 'Did—did my aunt and uncle know—how Fergus died?' Her eyes were pained.

'Yes,' he sighed. 'I had to tell them. The authorities were none too happy about having someone jump off one of their mountains, so they weren't broadcasting the fact that Fergus's death was anything but an accident, but just in case any of the media picked up on the truth . . . I had to tell your aunt and uncle, Lise,' he groaned. 'But they decided—and it had to be their decision—that you had adored Fergus too much to know the truth.'

'And instead I thought Fergus had found out about you and Terri and decided he didn't want to live without her.' She gave a pained frown. 'I'm sorry I thought that, Quinn,' and she hugged him tightly. 'I know you loved Fergus too, that you did all you could to help him.'

'It just wasn't enough,' he rasped.

'Darling, you did what you could.' She smoothed the pain from between his eyes.

'It wasn't enough,' he repeated harshly. 'And I

was never going to let another friend of mine die like that because I wasn't able to do anything to help them. Have you ever heard of FerMor Drug Rehabilitation Centres?' he frowned.

'No, I—*Fergus Mor*rison?' she realised dazedly.

'Hm,' Quinn nodded, his expression grim. 'I've managed to help them open several throughout North America.'

'By financing them with your concerts,' she guessed with self-contempt. And she had thought there had to be some sort of tax evasion involved! 'Marni told me that the money from those concerts goes to a "pet project" of yours,' she explained at his questioning look.

He gave a tight smile. 'It isn't much, but if I can help save one kid like Fergus then I'm satisfied.'

Quinn Taylor was a very special man, a man who came along only once in a lifetime, a man she would love and cherish for all her life.

'So what happens now?' she asked huskily.

He shook off his mood of despondency with an effort, his gaze warm as he smiled down at her. 'Now I marry the young girl who grew up into a princess?'

How apt, when she had thought of him as her Prince Charming from the moment they met!

'Yes, please,' she accepted eagerly.

His smile widened, his relief at her answer obvious. 'We're going to have to do *something* about your name,' he teased. 'Lise Morrison and Elizabeth Farnham will both have to go, much as I love them both. In future—in the very near future,' he amended arrogantly. 'You're going to become Lise Taylor.'

She finally knew exactly who she was, who she wanted to be for the rest of her life: the woman Quinn Taylor loved!

EPILOGUE

LISE had no idea how Cinderella had fared with her Prince Charming after the wedding, but there could be no doubt that the last four years with *her* Prince Charming had been magical!

They had waited only long enough for her grandfather to join them in Canada before being married, her grandfather staying on at the ranch to keep Marni company while Lise and Quinn went on their honeymoon. By the time they returned six weeks later she was already expecting their first child. Their second child had been born just a year after the first one, although they had waited another eighteen months before Lise discovered she was pregnant again.

She swung lazily back and forth in the swing-seat on the patio beside the house, smiling drowsily to herself as she waited for Quinn to finish his afternoon session in the studio.

'I think it's time all pregnant parents took a nap.'

She roused herself to look at her husband with a glowing smile. 'I thought you wouldn't be finished for hours yet.' She stood up to move into his waiting arms.

He grinned down at her. 'I shouldn't be,' he admitted ruefully. 'But the thought of the afternoon naps we've been taking while the girls have been away is very distracting!'

'The girls'. Daughters. They had three daughters: Marni, Claire, and Jennifer. Claire and Jennifer were spending the weekend with their indulgent grandparents on their farm, both Gayle and Dave Taylor doting on all their granddaughters. Marni would have probably been with her golden-haired two and three-year-old sisters if she hadn't been in England visiting with her 'Grandfather Farnham'. Marni spent a lot of time at Farnham Hall with her new grandfather, and Lise knew that Quinn was hoping she hadn't gone in search of that 'rich man who could give her a home like the Hall' now that she was nineteen. Lise happened to know, from a reliable source—Marni herself—that she had more than a passing interest in a fellow student at the college in Calgary that she attended. But she also like to tease Quinn, and Lise knew how much he liked to *be* teased by all his daughters.

'Grandfather has given strict instructions that *this* one is to be a boy,' she warned Quinn as his hand rested possessively against his child.

He shrugged. 'If it isn't we can always have another. And another. And another——'

'Quinn Taylor!' she cut in reprovingly.

'Hm?' He arched innocent brows, his eyes dancing with devilment.

For a moment Lise was lost in the beauty of his complete happiness, with her and their children. She had wanted so much to make him happy after all the unhappiness he had known, and she had only to look at him to know that together they had made *each other* happy.

'Lise?' he prompted again.

She gave him a glowing smile. 'Just how many children do we intend having?'

'Who's counting?' he asked, his head lowering to hers.

Who *was* counting? They could have a dozen children for all she cared, she loved being pregnant with, and having, Quinn's children. And the ease of her own pregnancies had told her that Maggie Taylor must have taken great care during her marriage to Quinn never to have his child. It made her all the more determined to surround him with a family that loved him.

'Don't worry, love,' Quinn teased as he pulled her towards their bedroom. 'You can't get pregnant when you're already pregnant! And you do need your nap,' he reminded her with exaggerated concern.

She laughed softly as they eagerly entered their bedroom. Perhaps it was as well she *couldn't* get pregnant at the moment, because after the long leisurely afternoons they had been spending in bed together—when they definitely *didn't* nap!—she had a feeling she soon would have been!

'Do you hear me protesting?' she said drily.

'I never do, love.' He softly closed the door behind them. 'I never do ...'

And she never would, she gave thanks every day of her life that she had Quinn to love, and to love her. She would never forget how close she came to forcing him from her for ever.

Her Prince Charming ...

Harlequin American Romance

Romances that go one step farther...
American Romance

Realistic stories involving people you can relate to and care about.

Compelling relationships between the mature men and women of today's world.

Romances that capture the core of genuine emotions between a man and a woman.

Join us each month for four new titles wherever paperback books are sold.
Enter the world of American Romance.

Harlequin Presents

COMING NEXT MONTH

1087 MY BROTHER'S KEEPER Emma Goldrick
Mickey is over the moon to have Harry home again. Life is good with her stepbrother around. Yet it's strange that she finds her thoughts centering less on her fiancé, George, and more on Harry....

1088 JENNY'S TURN Vanessa Grant
Making award-winning documentaries with Jake has been fun! However, when he declares his intention to marry her best friend, Jenny decides to leave. She'll never be one of Jake's women, but she can't stand the thought of him marrying someone else!

1089 FIGHT FOR LOVE Penny Jordan
When Natasha makes friends with an old Texas rancher in London, she never dreams that one day he'll leave her a legacy in his will. It isn't until she's at his ranch near Dallas that she begins to guess at his motives.

1090 FRAZER'S LAW Madeleine Ker
Rio enjoys studying the marine life off Australia's untamed Cape York Peninsula. She resents the intrusion of biologist Cameron Frazer into her remote solitude. But having to fight danger together makes her realize just how much they have in common.

1091 WHEN LOVERS MEET Flora Kidd
Jilly couldn't say that Ed Forster hadn't warned her. He'd made it very clear from the start that he wasn't interested in commitment. Recently widowed Jilly, however, isn't ready for a "torrid tropical affair"!

1092 NO MAN'S MISTRESS Roberta Leigh
A woman would have to be a real man-hater not to appreciate Benedict Peters—and Sara is no man-hater. Just the same she isn't going to join the admiring throng that sits at his feet—no matter how persuasive he is!

1093 REASONS OF THE HEART Susan Napier
Meeting Ross Tarrant brings Francesca's adolescent humiliation back with a jolt. Older and wiser now, successful in her way of life—surely she'll have the upper hand over the seemingly lackadaisical Ross. It just doesn't work out that way, though.

1094 DISHONOURABLE INTENTIONS Sally Wentworth
Rex Kynaston has everything it takes to attract a woman. The trouble is, he knows it. Not that it matters to Harriet. As far as she's concerned, he's the last man on earth she'd get involved with....

Available in July wherever paperback books are sold, or through Harlequin Reader Service:

In the U.S.
901 Fuhrmann Blvd.
P.O. Box 1397
Buffalo, N.Y. 14240-1397

In Canada
P.O. Box 603
Fort Erie, Ontario
L2A 5X3

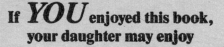